Blood Brotherhood

The Anglican Community of St Botolph's was very peaceful, high on the Yorkshire moors. Even its role of host to a small symposium on the role of the Church in the modern world was unlikely to disturb it, thought Father Anselm, head of the Community, as he gravely received his guests. They included a bishop who was a well-known TV personality; another from Africa who was black; three vicars, ranging from trendy to traditional; a non-denominational American with an interest in fund-raising; and – here the Father's gravity faltered a little – two Norwegian lady divines.

His composure was further shattered when he discovered one of his own community brutally murdered in his cell. Had the intrusion of the world, even in its least secular aspect, so far upset the Community as to release some pent-up love or hate? Or was it possible – though of course unthinkable – that one of the reverend visitors was handy with a knife? How could one conduct a murder enquiry in such a way that the image of Church and community was – well, not enhanced exactly, but at least decently preserved?

That problem soon troubled the distinguished visitors, not to mention the local police. Indeed, it so troubled one inspector that he shed further darkness on the scene. But the light, when it came, was blinding. It threatened a blaze of publicity, no less. How Father Anselm, the police and the distinguished visitors dealt with that delicate situation is urbanely and ironically revealed.

ROBERT BARNARD

Blood Brotherhood

COLLINS, ST JAMES'S PLACE, LONDON

William Collins Sons & Co Ltd
London · Glasgow · Sydney · Auckland
Toronto · Johannesburg

18000965

First published 1977
© Robert Barnard 1977

ISBN 0 00 231048 1
Set in Intertype Baskerville
Made and printed in Great Britain by
William Collins Sons & Co Ltd Glasgow

LH7 UP

CONTENTS

CHAPTER I

COMING

THE COMMUNITY of St Botolph's lies five miles from Hickley, in the West Riding of Yorkshire, set in rolling moorland country, glorious in summer, bleak in winter, and treacherous at all times. The walls of the Community stretch impressively far in all directions, and sheep belonging to the brothers graze both within and without them. Like all the other buildings within them, the walls are of comparatively recent date, having been built early in the present century, but they have already harmonized with their setting, and are often talked about by the younger locals as if they dated back to pre-Reformation times.

The locals, in fact, have very little to do with the Community, and know almost nothing about it. Now and then a taxi from Hickley station does the five-mile journey for the benefit of a solitary Anglican coming for a week or fortnight's retreat. The driver charges exorbitantly, for most of the retreaters are solidly middle-class, and don't like to haggle at the gate of one of the Lord's houses. Now and then, perhaps once a year, a larger retreat is arranged, a sort of symposium for ten or so participants, with a set topic for prayer, meditation and discussion, and then the taxis do good business, and use various dodges to drive the delegates out there singly, rather than in groups. The drivers report back to their wives that clerical gentlemen are notably careful in the matter of tipping, and that some prefer stepping it out on the windy moorland roads. And though the latter gentlemen probably think this walking admirably consonant with their pastoral function, the wives shake their heads, and say that the clergy have sadly declined in class over the past few years.

It was such a symposium, attended by Anglicans and fraternal delegates from other parts of the world, that took place at the Community of St Botolph's in the last week of July, when the heather lay like a purple blanket over the moorlands, and a large proportion of the local population were baking uncomfortably and loathing the food on the Costa del Sol.

The Right Reverend Henry Caradyce Forde, Bishop of Peckham and Dulwich, looked what he was : a bishop in the prime of life. He had reached the age of heart attacks and thoughts of mortality without it having any radical effect on his temper. He gazed out on the world, bland, benign, and sceptical.

The world, in the present instance, was a first-class compartment on the train that was taking him on the first leg of his journey to Hickley and the Community of St Botolph's. But he was not observing it. As usual when he looked most benign, his thoughts were elsewhere. Usually he was planning the next chapter in one of the little paperback volumes in which he questioned – gently, quizzically, devastatingly – every aspect of conventional Anglican faith, volumes which had brought down on his head the righteous anger of the *Sunday Express*. Today he was composing a short opening speech for one of the discussion sessions at St Botolph's.

The subject for the week-long symposium had appealed to him : 'The Social Role of the Church in the Modern World.' It had presented, it seemed to him, unlimited opportunities for dressing up truisms to look like paradoxes, as well as the chance to make some agreeably sly references to the present Archbishop of Canterbury. The speech, which should be as informal as possible, blossomed in his fertile brain.

'At first sight,' he said to himself, 'it would seem paradoxical that we should meet to discuss the social role of the Church in the midst of a community which has with-

drawn itself from the world, has said, in effect, that it wants
nothing to do with it. Yet is it, after all, so paradoxical?'

He paused, dissatisfied. Too much like an address, a
sermon. How difficult it was to get out of the habit of
sermonizing. But this was to be an informal group, meeting
for discussion and prayer. Something less well-phrased was
called for. He prepared to remove the clerical stilts from
his phraseology, but he was distracted by some stirrings in
his vicinity. He knew the signs, and with an inaudible sigh
he returned to the present.

He was not alone in his compartment, and he had pur-
posely given no greeting or encouragement to converse
when he got into it to the other occupant, who was a
muddly, middle-aged woman of the sort who is invariably
attracted to clergymen, without being attractive to them.
He had not expected a totally silent journey, but he had
hoped for a rather longer period of meditation before he
was interrupted.

'You will excuse me speaking, won't you?' said the lady,
flustered, and patting purposelessly the various items of
luggage that were scattered around her. 'I wouldn't have
done as a rule, of course, but I saw you were a clergyman.'

The Bishop was peeved. 'A clergyman', indeed! He had
assumed she had recognized him. She should have recognized him. What *was* the use of all those television engage-
ments if people didn't know who you were? He suppressed
his bile, however, and smiled benevolently at her.

'It's just that I have been *so* troubled recently, and I'm
alone, you see, no one to talk it over with, and it would be
such a relief – it's Cassandra, you see, my pussy, she died,
and – '

Oh, Lord, mused the Bishop, it's the one about whether
animals can go to heaven. It was one of the most common
subjects for spirit-wrestling among the laity, and he was
accustomed, in such cases, to administer comfort rather
than theology, because comfort was quicker. He therefore
interrupted the flow of her discourse to reassure her.

'Not beyond the bounds of hope . . . God in His infinite mercy . . . It may well be that a place will be found for a beloved pet . . .'

The smooth phrases flowed automatically, and it was only after some time that he realized that the woman was looking at him with an expression of puzzlement on her face. He stopped in his tracks.

'But I've never had any difficulty in believing animals can go to heaven,' said the woman with unusual force. 'I've always found it much more difficult to believe human beings go there. No, my problem is quite different . . .'

As she resumed her flow, the Bishop sighed again, this time not quite silently.

The Reverend Stewart Phipps, vicar of St Luke's, Blackburn, cycled in the direction of Hickley. He was a practised, passionate pedaller, and his thin body put into this activity the same sort of burning zeal that he had put into everything he did since he had become a Christian at the age of fourteen.

His conversion had taken place in King's College Chapel, on a sunny spring day, at dusk, and at the time he had been inclined to ceremony, pageantry and Roman theatricals. He had even believed passionately in the celibacy of the clergy. Some years later, in his late teens, he had felt stirrings in himself which he suspected strongly to be the sexual instinct. After agonies of conscience he came to rearrange his priorities, and a new passion took hold of his lean, wiry frame : radical politics. It was his fiery (indeed tedious) devotion to all known causes of the left, and a good many of his own devising, that had persuaded his superiors to send him to the industrial North for his first preferment, though he himself was from Surbiton.

It had not been a happy choice. The parishioners of St Luke's had not welcomed young Phipps's determination to use the pulpit to elaborate on themes which he had already taken up in letters published and unpublished to *Peace*

News, Tribune, and the *Morning Star.* Far from it. They themselves voted Conservative, when they did not vote National Front, and they did not believe in mixing any politics except their own with religion. Their anger and contempt acted like a drug on the young Reverend Phipps : he only thrived on opposition. He had flung in their faces terms like 'bourgeois democracy', 'freedom fighters', 'the corruption of the masses' and any other catch-phrase which came to hand, especially any that could express his infinite contempt for them, their opinions and their way of life. And he did it with such icy oratorical gusto that his parishioners, groping for comparisons, came up most frequently with the names of John Calvin and Michael Foot. The high point of his incumbency to date had been his call to the congregation to offer their prayers for the work of the Baader-Meinhof gang, when the half-empty church had emptied itself in seconds. What a glorious triumph that had been!

Memories of the outrage on the faces of the parishioners as they left the church brought a near-smile of pleasure to the face of Stewart Phipps, but the lighting-up was momentary. For the rest he pedalled on concentratedly in the direction of Hickley, his eyes aglow with faith and Socialism.

In his little Mini, speeding bumpily from his draughty rectory in the depths of Lincolnshire towards Hickley and the Community of St Botolph's, the Reverend Ernest Clayton had a problem not unlike that of the Bishop of Peckham. He had picked up a hitch-hiker – something he did fairly frequently, for the bulk of his congregation was on the wrong side of fifty, and he missed the contact with the young, or told himself that he missed it. He certainly felt rather younger than most of his parishioners : he was a spare, vigorous man, and had a puckish expression that made him look like the sort of cleric that used to be portrayed in films by Wilfred Hyde-White. When people said he had a wicked look in his eye, though, they meant no more than that he had a sharp sense of humour.

That sense of humour was being tried to the uttermost at the moment. The hitch-hiker had turned out to be a young man (you never knew) of around twenty, wearing the regulation clothes of his generation and sporting the regulation non-hair-cut. The oldest thing about his person seemed to be his knapsack, which bore approved slogans from the last twenty years all over it, from 'Make Love Not War' (a foolish commandment, Ernest Clayton thought, since people through the ages had so conspicuously managed to combine both activities), through various ecological pieties, to some recent ones that he tried not to read. The boy's face was that of a corrupted cherub, an idea accentuated by the thick halo of fair hair. And he was insisting on talking about religion.

He put himself up, as young people often do, as the spokesman for his generation. What I think, everybody thinks, he seemed to say. He spoke in an incongruous public school accent – incongruous because, to someone of the Reverend Clayton's generation, a public school accent implied certain clothes, certain standards, certain destinations in life, all of which gave the possessor an accepted place in a clergyman's *Almanach de Gotha*. This young man certainly occupied no such place, and neither was his religion any of the accepted brands. It was a mish-mash of Shelley and Lawrence, dredged through the minds of various American poets and popular sages – a series of diktats of permissiveness which at best seemed a form of gross self-indulgence, and at worst a determination to wallow in vileness for its own sake.

'If you did but know it, the only sin is self-repression,' said the boy, turning his big blue eyes in the direction of the Reverend Clayton to see what effect his effusions were having, and allowing a knowing smile to play around his lips. 'If you want to do a thing, you've got to follow the impulse through right to the end of the road, because if you stop yourself you're killing something – it's worse than murder, because you're killing part of yourself.'

From this odd statement of values, the cherub went on to his view of the after life, the spiritual value of various drugs which enabled you to enjoy premature participation in the hereafter, and various other matters too abstruse or jargon-bound to hold the Reverend Clayton's attention. Why on earth, he thought to himself, does everyone think they have to talk religion when they meet a clergyman? If you meet a plumber, you don't feel you have to talk about plumbing. Then the thought struck him that when he met a plumber he generally *did* talk about plumbing, since that in his rectory was primitive in the extreme and had to be fixed by himself, his stipend not running to the sort of professional attention it obviously needed.

He wafted his attention back towards the grubby Shelley in the passenger seat beside him, who seemed to have sensed that he had lost his audience. He had let a pout appear on his unpleasantly full lips during a pause for thought, and he had then turned to the subject of sex, as a sure-fire recipe for getting back his listener's attention.

'Your generation got hung-up on sex,' he jeered.

'Well, we certainly didn't talk about it quite so much as yours,' murmured the Reverend Clayton.

'You thought about it more, though. Nasty little secret thoughts.' (The Reverend Clayton wondered whether he was right, but found he really couldn't remember.) 'My generation's had to do what your lot only thought of doing, and wanted to do, and didn't dare. And we've done a few things you didn't even dream possible too. Your lot lived their lives in one long wet wank.' He turned round with a taunting smile. 'You might say you didn't have the courage of your - - - - convictions.'

He had used the gerundival form of a four-letter word which in the Reverend Clayton's youth would only have been heard by those unfortunate young clerics who opted or were sent to carry the faith into the more savage parts

of London's East End. Ernest Clayton pressed his right
foot down on the brake, leaned over the be-jeaned and
sweat-shirted figure beside him, and opened the passenger
door.

'Get out,' he said.

'What do you mean?' protested the young man, with his
evil-choirboy smile. 'You said you were going to Hickley.
I'm going to Hickley. What's gotten into you?'

The Reverend Clayton summoned up the authority of
years in the pulpit and as chairman of frequently acri-
monious committee and board meetings.

'Out,' he said, 'before I throw you.'

Rather to his surprise, the cherub obeyed. With a con-
temptuous laugh to hide any disappointment he might feel,
he slouched out, and banged the door to. As he started his
Mini in motion, Ernest Clayton bent towards the open
window, and shouted: 'I was just obeying my impulse,
you know, just obeying my impulse.'

As he drove down the road, he saw the fair-haired figure
take up his position by the side of the road again. He had
to admit that he hadn't felt so pleased with himself for a
long time.

The Bishop of Mitabezi sat on his aisle seat in the Boeing
727 that was carrying him from the World Council of
Churches meeting in Geneva to London, there to change
planes for the North of England and, ultimately, by car,
for the Community of St Botolph's at Hickley. The Bishop
was as near asleep as made no difference, but his fleshy,
substantial, episcopal frame still seemed impressive and
powerful, as it chafed against the confines of his plane seat.

The meeting had been a success, that was certain, and a
feeling of personal achievement pervaded his somnolent
form: large sums of money had been voted to various
African independence groups, guerrilla fighters struggling
to establish legitimate black oppressions; many passionate
and blood-thirsty speeches had been made; the Anglican

representative from the mother country had been positively apologetic in all the speeches he made about racial matters, and his lead had been followed by most of the European delegates except the Scandinavians, who were too smug on the subject of race to be apologetic. In fact, as far as he was concerned, a jolly good time had been had by all.

There had been some theology talked too, and here the Bishop never felt at his happiest. But he had, surprisingly, made a considerable impact with a speech towards the end of a debate concerning certain niceties of the communion service, where he had described himself as a worker and a teacher, rather than a thinker, and had appealed for brotherhood and unity and Christian charity and all manner of goodies. Perhaps it was the contrast with his strident truculence in the earlier sessions that had made the delegates receive his speech with a gentle hum of approval. How fortunate that much of the speech could be given again, almost word for word, to the delegates at the St Botolph's symposium!

As he drifted off into total sleep, fragments of the meetings he had just attended, impressions of the world around him, and anticipations for the future merged in his mind:

'Our brothers in Christ fighting for their independence in . . . legs . . . the body and blood of Our Saviour . . . white legs . . . death to the white oppressors . . . air-hostess's legs . . . blood and devastation . . . the body and blood of Our Lord . . . blood and fire . . . blood . . .'

On the second-class seat sat the travelling clergyman, his ticket protruding from the breast pocket of his once-smart corduroy jacket, and his keys jingling in his twill trousers. He might have been thought less fortunate than the Bishop of Peckham, for he was surrounded by Liverpudlian youth, all travelling, like him, towards Yorkshire. But, far from minding, he seemed to be revelling in their talk.

Philip Lambton was a clergyman for the young. He was, he thought, young himself, or youngish. Thirty-seven was

no age these days, and he had the happy ability not to look
ahead to thirty-eight, thirty-nine. He had a child-like faith
in what he was doing, and an enviable faculty of shrugging
off unfortunate consequences without a shadow of effort.
He loved – innocently – publicity, and he collected his
cuttings like any rep. actor.

He had just had a great success. His church, St Finian's,
in one of the suburbs of Liverpool, had been the setting
(thanks entirely to his efforts) for the performance of a rock
Te Deum, performed by a group called the Grots, and
composed by their lead guitarist. He had culled texts from
the Bible, the Hindu sages, and William Burroughs, and
set them to an ear-splitting score that made all the houses
in the vicinity of St Finian's near-uninhabitable for days
during the rehearsals and performances. The young of the
parish, many of whom had not shown their noses in church
since their forcible christenings, had been recruited to
bellow various simple phrases in chorus. And there had
been an awful lot of publicity.

The Reverend Lambton's face lit up in a child-like smile
as he thought of how much there had been. The local
papers had been full of it for weeks in advance, and one
had had a whole-page interview with him, in which he had
quoted the injunction to 'Suffer little children' (ignoring
the fact that most of the performers were disconcertingly
unchild-like). Then there had been the interview on the
Today programme – surely the high-spot of his ministry
to date. True, it had been cut to a minute and a quarter,
and had included only his reply to the local critics and not
his disquisition on the spiritual content of the work itself.
This had made him sound defensive, which was a pity. But
still, the BBC was the BBC – undoubtedly a National
Forum. And the contacts he had made would be put to
very good use in the future.

Of course there had been critics. Those who tried to do
the work of the Lord in a modern, relevant, meaningful
way, a way that spoke to today's generation (he'd used all

these phrases in the bit cut out of the broadcast) must expect ridicule and opposition. People had come along complaining about the pervasive odour in the vestry, which they said was certainly not incense. Then there had been the old woman who maintained she saw the Grots' drummer urinating in the font. What fools these people made of themselves! Besides, they were the dying generations. His business was with the young in one another's arms.

He was in the middle of a fatuous reverie, in which his own role hovered between that of boy bishop and leader of a new children's crusade, when he heard the words 'Rock Te Deum' from the mouth of the youth next to him. He jerked to attention.

'Dragsville,' said the girl opposite, pulling down the edges of her mouth, and uttering a groan. The rest of the group sniggered, and went on to other matters.

A cloud seemed to have passed over the blue of Philip Lambton's heaven.

All these, and others, were heading towards the Community of St Botolph's, and towards the strange events that took place there in the late, hot days of July.

CHAPTER II

ASSEMBLING

THE BISHOP OF Peckham floated blandly from his carriage on the little local train from Leeds to Hickley and bestowed his ticket on the ticket collector as reverently as if it were a communion wafer. He was, in fact, thinking up jokes for his speech.

Once outside the station, his sense of the practicalities of life reasserted itself. His eye took in the grey-brown stone of Hickley, cast a glance of pastoral approval on the moorlands visible above the roof-tops, and then surveyed the waiting taxis. He turned around to appraise his fellow passengers who had got off with him. Most were bustling off towards town and home, but one was eyeing him hesitantly, as if uncertain whether to make the first gesture of approach. He was a tall, weighty young man, over-scrubbed and dressed in a light-weight suit, perilously close to sky-blue in colour. Probably American, thought the Bishop. Or, worse, Canadian. Still, it would halve the cost of the trip, however boring the conversation.

'Are you for St Botolph's?' boomed the Bishop, and receiving a gesture of assent he ushered the eager young cleric towards the first of the waiting taxis.

'I deeply appreciate your gesture,' intoned the young man. 'A truly Christian act.'

The Bishop had a sinking feeling that he was going to get the boring conversation without halving the cost of the fare.

This feeling was augmented as the taxi got under way. After introductions had been expansively performed the young man – whose name was Simeon P. Fleishman – began talking about the absorbing topic of the price of his

rail ticket from London, doing laborious calculations involving different rates of exchange for the dollar. This done,
he turned to the equally fascinating subject of fund-raising.

It soon turned out that, to the Reverend Fleishman, the
social role of the Church in the modern world meant little
more than ways of screwing money out of the congregation,
ways which were – even to so modern a bishop as the
Bishop of Peckham – breathtaking in their grasp of the
principles of high finance, in their capitalist daring, and
in their sheer rapacity.

'We believe,' mouthed the Reverend Fleishman earnestly,
'that since God's day is one seventh of the full week, true
Christians should be willing to donate to their place of
worship one-seventh of their weekly income.'

'Good God,' said the Bishop. 'And do they?'

'There is some reluctance to acknowledge the full spiritual
force of the argument,' admitted Simeon P., 'but we are
unremitting in getting the message across, and it's gratifying
to be able to report that some do, some do.'

'You must be rolling,' said the Bishop, who enjoyed cal-
culated descents into the vernacular. 'What on earth do
you do with it all?'

A shade flitted briefly over the piercingly honest eyes of
the Reverend Fleishman.

'It goes to the refurbishment of the edifice,' he said,
'and to the enhancement of the community appeal of our
particular Christian message.'

Flim-flam, said the Bishop to himself. Aloud he asked:
'And your church is . . . er . . . the Episcopalian?'

'We call ourselves the Church of the Risen Jesus,' said
the young man, 'but basically we're non-denominational.'

The subject was one of great appeal (and some suspicion)
to the Bishop, but he was prevented from making any
theological explorations of Simeon P. Fleishman's faith
by their arrival outside the impressive wooden gate of St
Botolph's. While the young man looked on disinterestedly
the Bishop haggled over the exorbitant fare, got it reduced

by twenty per cent, and added no tip. The scruples of the middle-class laity were not for him, and he was sure that the Lord (to use a convenient formula) would be no more pleased to see His servants swindled outside His door than any other good host. Finally he emerged from the taxi with a benign sense of good work done, and a nagging feeling that he ought to have had his share of the American's non-denominational pickings.

As the taxi driver did a disgruntled U-turn and drove off, the Bishop and Simeon P. stood for a few moments in silence, stretching their legs in the sunshine and gazing along the impressive length of the Community walls, winding their irregular way across the purple moorlands almost as far as the eye could see.

'This sure is peaceful,' said the Reverend Fleishman in a reverent tone. 'Mighty peaceful. Kind of medieval.'

'Edwardian, dear boy, if not later,' said the Bishop firmly. 'A refuge from guzzling and womanizing.'

'That would be Edward the . . .' said the Reverend Fleishman tentatively, obviously wanting to get things right for some future edition of his parish magazine or company statement. But the Bishop decided he had had enough, and tugged at the bell.

As they waited in the heat, they were joined by a lean and hungry-looking figure which pedalled furiously up to the gate and dismounted from his cycle with almost military precision. Stewart Phipps shook hands briefly with the two of them, obviously recognizing the Bishop (who flirted with all the political parties, and occasionally contributed witty and paradoxical pieces to some of the same journals as the Reverend Phipps, though the editors never regarded his pieces as sufficiently committed, and only printed them on account of his mitre). This done, Stewart Phipps stood a little aside, eyeing Simeon P. from his sharp, hooded eyes, which proclaimed with anticipation: An American. He'll have to defend himself all right. What shall I get him on? Vietnam; CIA; Ronald Reagan; Greece; Watergate;

able : he seemed to see, without offering anything of himself to be seen. His voice when he spoke was quiet, baritone rather than the expected bass, but strong and individual.

'You are all most welcome,' he said, looking from one to the other as if registering through them how the world was progressing.

'I'm sure we're going to find it a remarkably interesting experience being here,' said the Bishop (unaware how truly he spoke). 'I presume our American friend here is not too well acquainted with communities of this sort.'

'I hope we can provide a congenial atmosphere for your discussions,' said Father Anselm, half inclining his head towards Simeon Fleishman. 'These symposia are valuable times for us, though infrequent.'

'It sure is peaceful here,' said Fleishman, who seemed unable to get beyond that simple idea. Father Anselm bowed his distinguished head gravely, and no one saw his mouth twitch.

'I gather some members of the Community will be joining us in our discussions, is that not so? We'll look forward to that,' said the Bishop. His manner was breezy, less intimidated than the others by Father Anselm's awesome presence.

'Yes, one or two who have shown a special interest. I hope they will be able to bring a slightly different perspective from the other participants.' Father Anselm paused. 'I trust you will forgive what you may regard as naïvety, even ignorance. We are, as you will understand, very cut off here at St Botolph's.'

As the Reverend Fleishman seemed again about to comment on the peace of the place, as if he'd expected something more like a railway terminal, the Bishop cut in with : 'But of course you in this order are not entirely shut off from the world, are you?'

'No, no,' said Father Anselm. 'The brothers may, at certain hours on one day of the week, go outside. But few do. I myself take a newspaper to keep some contact with the world around me, and anyone may borrow that. Few do. We are, you may say, closed by choice rather than by our vows. Hence, as I say, our views may seem to you naïve or ill-informed.' He paused and looked around them, and seemed to register that they were all, especially the Reverend Phipps, somewhat travel-stained. 'But I forget, you will want to go to your rooms. Perhaps we may meet in the chapel for Evensong at five o'clock.

He rang a little bell, and another brother, younger than the first, fair-haired and stern, came from an inner room and led the way out to the corridor again. As they left, Father Anselm again inclined his head, and no one seemed quite sure what to do in reply.

'Goodness me,' said the Bishop, who had been more impressed by the interview than he liked to be by his fellow-churchmen. 'There is something medieval about it, after all.'

Ernest Clayton was feeling moderately full of well-being: he had enjoyed his first sight of St Botolph's and its glorious position; he had enjoyed – for a rectory in Lincolnshire offers few opportunities for novelty and surprise – his meeting with Father Anselm; he had liked his simple cell-like room, with its narrow bed and two shelves, nothing more; he had enjoyed the singing of Evensong in the austere but elegant chapel. And now he was rather enjoying the little gathering that was to lead to the first meal in that splendid dining-hall.

True, Philip Lambton wouldn't have been the first choice to chat to as a general rule, with his fatuous cult of youth, which seemed more than ever foolish to the Reverend Clayton after his experience with the hitch-hiker that morning. Still, at least one knew to avoid him in future – unless, as sometimes happened at gatherings of churchmen, everyone else proved equally avoid-worthy. But surely this was not likely to prove the case this time? Father Anselm was clearly an interesting man, if he would come down off his

spiritual mountain; the Bishop of Peckham was (to put it
no higher) a sprightly mind, and one met few enough of
those these days; the Bishop of Mitabezi, even, offered the
prospect of an interesting chat to one whose parents had
been missionaries, and whose earliest memories were of
scrubbed mission-houses in India and congregations in incongruous dark suits and pinafores. The Reverend Clayton
clutched his glass, which contained a barley drink that was
far from unpleasant, and might with luck turn out to be
mildly alcoholic, and decided that he had a lot to be
thankful for.

They were gathered in one of the smaller rooms, sepa-
rated from the dining-hall only by a couple of archways:
through them he could see the brothers congregating before
their meal, some apparently chatting brightly to each other,
others seemingly sunk in meditation. There were three
brothers in the side room with the delegates to the symposium: one was Brother Dominic, the fair young man
who had shown him and the other delegates to their rooms
– polite but unforthcoming, with cold eyes; the second
was the one who had met him at the gate, a nondescript
man in his late thirties, weak-eyed and round-bellied; the
third was very old indeed, and seemed more than a little
unsure of what was going on. What could he contribute
to a symposium on the role of the Church in the Modern
World, the Reverend Clayton wondered?

He tore himself away from Philip Lambton, who had
launched into an account of further plans to desecrate his
church in the cause of adolescence, and turned to the
young brother who was standing near, slightly apart, and
quite self-contained.

'Remarkably pleasant surroundings you have here,' he
said.

'We think so,' said Brother Dominic. Both lapsed into
silence.

'I suppose we are not really seeing them as they usually
are, though,' said Ernest Clayton.

'No, no,' said the young man, 'things are very different as a rule.' He seemed to be holding something back – perhaps that he heartily wished them all gone. In which case, why was he participating in the symposium?

'How do you spend the greater part of your day?' asked Clayton. 'How do you divide it up?'

'Most of it in prayer or work. But of course we also have the various observances, and we converse before meals.'

'Are you quiet for most of the time, then?'

'Yes, by choice. We have no definite rule, but we mostly prefer to keep our conversation for those times.'

'A lonely life.'

'Perhaps, from one point of view,' said the young man, who seemed prepared to give information, but remained non-committal whenever any expression of opinion seemed called for.

'Why do people come here?'

'Many reasons. As many reasons as we have brothers, perhaps. But we don't pry into each other's reasons. We would only talk about that if a brother desired to unburden himself.'

'I see, yes,' said Ernest Clayton, finding the young man an oddly unsatisfying companion. Since he volunteered nothing further, Clayton was obliged to turn back to the clerical impresario of St Finian's.

'I think you'll find,' said Simeon P. Fleishman, with a lumbering patience, 'that every single decent American citizen found the Watergate business deeply disturbing. Deeply disturbing. I think I may say they were quite as shocked as you were over here in Europe.'

'Poppycock!' spat out Stewart Phipps. 'You all elected that crook with a record majority six months after the thing broke. I bet you voted for him yourself.'

'I feel that every man's vote is a matter between . . .'

'I thought so. The point about Watergate that you haven't understood yet is that it's not just the Nixon crew who were implicated. It was every single American.'

'I don't quite accept your premise there, Mr ... er ... Phitts, and I must say that every American I know is bored to death with the whole Watergate business by now.'

'All right. Then take the CIA ...'

With a sigh Simeon P. Fleishman prepared to take on himself the responsibility for having tried to poison Fidel Castro's cigars.

The two bishops were very genial together.

'Been rabble-rousing in Geneva, I take it?' said he of Peckham.

'I have been doing my bit, yes,' said he of Mitabezi.

'Screwing money out of us for terrorists by making us feel guilty, I suppose?' said Peckham.

'I rather think the Anglican delegation came feeling guilty already,' said Mitabezi, with a glint in his eye.

'No doubt. Led by Dilchester, weren't they? No backbone. No love of the fight. I shudder to think what the people who write to *The Times* will say.'

'I wonder whether we don't pay too much attention to the people who write to *The Times*,' said Ernest Clayton, who had detached himself from his ecclesiastical Lew Grade and had joined the group.

'What else can we do?' said the Bishop of Peckham, with a nod to acknowledge Clayton's existence and right to join the discussion. 'They're the only people who still come to church.'

'I wonder why we do so much worse than other countries,' said Ernest Clayton with a little bow in the direction of the Bishop of Mitabezi. 'Our figures for regular worshippers are a positive embarrassment.'

'Too many television channels,' said the Bishop of Peckham. 'It's all a question of the amount of competition.'

'The Americans do much better, and they have more,' Ernest Clayton pointed out.

'We in Africa believe the English went lazy when they

lost their Empire,' said the Bishop of Mitabezi. 'Perhaps that has had its effect on church attendance too.'

'You may well have a point there,' said Clayton. 'Post-imperial lethargy. And then of course there are all the people who blame the welfare state.'

'Interesting to hear from the Scandinavians on that,' said the Bishop of Peckham. 'I wonder they're not here.'

'I believe it was rough on the North Sea today,' said Ernest Clayton. 'That could have delayed them if they were coming that way. Where exactly are they from?'

They consulted their typewritten list of delegates.

'Both from Norway,' said the Bishop of Peckham. 'No doubt that's how they are coming. What odd names: Bente Frøystad – very curious. I suppose it's the same as the Swedish Bengt. I remember several Bengts when we had the World Council meetings in Sweden.'

'The other is even more unfortunate,' said Ernest Clayton.

'Randi Paulsen,' said the Bishop of Peckham, with a great belly laugh. 'Oh, goodness me, how unsuitable! Fancy a man going through life with a name like Randi?'

'A woman,' said a clear soprano voice behind him – quite softly, but it brought a sudden deathly hush to the whole assembly. The Bishop slowly wheeled himself round to face the arch opening into the dining-hall.

Framed in the archway his eye caught, first of all, Father Anselm, whose grave aplomb seemed for once to be somewhat ruffled, and then the members of the Norwegian delegation. There could be no doubt that not one, but both, were of the female sex.

CHAPTER III

MEN AND WOMEN

FATHER ANSELM led the Norwegian delegation first to the Bishop of Peckham, who gave them a look of puckish delight. Father Anselm regarded him sourly, and almost immediately went into a huddle with Brother Dominic by one of the arches leading to the main hall. The Norwegian delegation then proceeded round the group, introducing themselves, and finally landed up under the benign bulk of the Bishop of Mitabezi, who seemed quite unembarrassed by their arrival, and perhaps even appreciative. The rest of the delegates took their first relaxed intake of breath since the newcomers had appeared in the doorway and began to think over their position. Brother Dominic had now disappeared, and, responding to an infinitesimal nod from Father Anselm, the Bishop of Peckham glided out into the great hall, where they put themselves in a corner out of sight of the delegates, though not of the assembled brothers, who were looking in their direction with considerable curiosity evident on their faces.

'You realize,' said Father Anselm urgently, 'that the presence of women within the Community's walls is totally against all the rules of our order – and absolutely unprecedented?'

'Of course, my dear chap, naturally,' said the Bishop, rather surprised at having to soothe the awesome head of the Community. 'But it's Church House you must quarrel with, you know. I've had nothing to do with making up the list of delegates.'

'I quite understand that,' said Father Anselm, obviously struggling to regain total equanimity. 'But Church House said that you were to be regarded as the unofficial leader of the symposium. I look to you to make a decision as to what we should do, now that they are here.'

The Bishop pondered for a moment. The situation appealed greatly to his sense of humour, and to his sense of the dramatic too (he was a governor of the National Theatre, and had always taken the lead in his theological college's annual play). The situation was pregnant with further piquant possibilities, and really there seemed no good reason why, once there, the newcomers should not be allowed to remain.

'We should look terrible fools if we just told them to leave,' he said. 'Think how the Sunday papers would laugh if they got hold of it. Surely there can be no harm in their staying?'

'I give no opinion on that,' said Father Anselm, compressing his thin lips. 'I merely ask for directions. What are we to do with them, if they are allowed to stay?'

'You haven't shown them to their rooms?' Father Anselm shook his head, a pained expression on his face. 'I suppose we could always find them rooms in Hickley,' the Bishop mused.

'Perhaps,' said Father Anselm; 'but the sort of comment that would be aroused might be regrettable.'

'Of course, of course. Having them coming and going every day for the discussions would be worse than having them here all the time. Well, as far as I can see, the best thing to do would be to treat them like any other delegate, and square it with your flock.' He gestured in the direction of the little groups of brothers, who quickly turned their heads away, as if oblivious of their presence.

'Put them in the visitors' wing, do you mean?' said Father Anselm. 'With the rest of the delegates?'

'Well, after all, why not?' said the Bishop. 'Damn it all, we *are* clergymen.'

Ernest Clayton had watched the arrival and introduction of the Norwegian delegation with a rich amusement that he did not allow to spread beyond his eyes. The reactions of the other participants in the symposium had been a picture, for an amateur in human nature like himself: the dim, elderly brother had regarded them with a bemused horror, as if they were the culmination of a series of shocks with which the modern world had battered his old head; the other brothers had looked sour and suspicious; the American had not seemed to register that there was anything amiss, while Stewart Phipps and Philip Lambton, who obviously knew the rules of the place, had both seemed rather pleased than otherwise; the Bishop of Mitabezi had beamed an even more unambiguous welcome and had then taken them spontaneously under his wing, especially Bente Frøystad.

For although the Norwegian delegation were both female, one member was undoubtedly more female than the other. Bente Frøystad was a healthy girl with a splendid figure, and a forthright, determined manner. Her open face owed nothing to make-up and everything to a good constitution and plenty of exercise. One could understand the Bishop's frank, boyish appreciation, though one also got the impression that she was a girl of very decided views, one whom it would not do to cross, either in an argument or a fight.

Randi Paulsen on the other hand . . . The Reverend Clayton considered. She seemed to be a variant of a type he knew in England, a type that had been more frequent in his youth than it was today. Frøken Paulsen was pinched and angular, and carried herself with a stiff correctness about the shoulders, as if she wanted you to forget that she had a body. She wore a cardigan and skirt in the sort of pretty pastel shade much favoured by women's magazines twenty years ago. Her face was small and forgettable, but she wore the expression of self-satisfaction affected by the unco guid, and her eyes shone with suspicion of the intentions of men.

Both girls affected to be quite unconscious that their presence in the Community was in any way unusual, but

Ernest Clayton felt sure that both were perfectly well aware of the fact – and he suspected that they were both enjoying it, in different ways.

'We in Norway are very conscious of the needs of the developing nations,' Randi Paulsen was saying virtuously in her correct, lifeless English to the Bishop of Mitabezi, who was looking at Bente Frøystad. 'We in my own parish have collected several thousand crowns, and we have adopted a mission school and a hospital in Africa. It gives everyone in the parish such a special interest in your continent, and it is so sweet to be able to tell the little ones in my Sunday class . . .'

But she was interrupted in mid-sweetness and light by Father Anselm, who had returned with the Bishop of Peckham, and now sternly proposed to show them to their rooms. Ernest Clayton could see that the Bishop of Peckham was thoroughly delighted by the whole business.

'Quite a turn-up for the book, eh?' he boomed at the Bishop of Mitabezi. 'That dented our friend Anselm's gravity, what?'

'A very pleasant surprise,' said Mitabezi.

'Especially one of them, eh? But we'll have to be discreet, you know – ' at this point he broke off, seeing an expression of naïve protest on the Bishop of Mitabezi's face, as if he had been suspected of contemplating something he hadn't even begun to contemplate. 'I don't mean in conduct, of course,' said the Bishop of Peckham hurriedly, looking round appealingly to all the other delegates, 'that goes without saying – no, I mean we'll have to be discreet when we get outside again. Mum's the word, you know. The papers would laugh themselves silly if they got hold of it. The fact is, Church House has made a frightful bloomer, perfectly frightful, and I'm going to have to blow them up in no uncertain terms when I get back to London. It's lucky it's they who've made asses of themselves, but that is all the more reason to be discreet.'

They all nodded sagely, though Clayton was still not

sure whether Simeon P. Fleishman had understood. He had just stood there through the speech looking solid, earnest, and – yes, sinister. Then Clayton's eyes were caught by the elderly brother, standing unnoticed in a corner. His eyes were still dim and bleary, his hearing apparently uncertain, but he seemed about to come forward and make a protest : he had raised his hands in a gesture of distress and had taken a step forward when the middle-aged brother, his face expressing friendly concern, went over to him, drew him away into a corner, and apparently soothed him. The incident went quite unnoticed by the rest of the delegates.

Shortly afterwards the Norwegian contingent returned, and a great bell clanged for dinner.

The meal was only a moderate success, the Reverend Clayton thought. The guest table was set on a dais at some distance from the rows of tables occupied by the resident brothers, but all the guests were conscious of a wave of – something – disapproval perhaps? wafting in their direction. The brothers, who had been talked to by their spiritual leader, seemed quite ostentatiously unaware of the alien presences at the guest table, though Clayton's sharp eyes caught one or two surreptitious peeps in that direction. Father Anselm, after asking the Bishop of Peckham to say grace, remained silent for much of the rest of the meal, in dignified disapproval.

Randi Paulsen was seated next to the Bishop of Mitabezi. This was not at all how he had planned things. He had done his best to secure Bente Frøystad, but he had been outmanoeuvred by the Bishop of Peckham. Mitabezi had taken his defeat in a Christian spirit, merely vowing that he wouldn't be outdone again by that sort of nifty footwork. Meanwhile he smiled benignly on Frøken Paulsen, who was still on the subject of the developing nations, and was giving an all-too-full account of Norwegian missions in various unattractive parts of the globe.

When her sacchrine monotone finally faded into silence,

the Reverend Stewart Phipps, who was seated on her left, said in his harsh voice : 'And how many coloured immigrants have you in Norway?'

'As many as we can absorb,' said Randi Paulsen virtuously. 'At the moment we have a complete ban on immigration, until we can ensure a proper standard of housing and so on for every immigrant. We feel sure this is the most responsible approach.'

'Charity begins abroad, obviously,' said Stewart Phipps. 'A new variant of telescopic philanthropy, that.'

Randi Paulsen looked at him uncomprehendingly.

The Bishop of Peckham was getting on much better with Bente Frøystad – so well as to arouse some resentment in the breast of Philip Lambton, who was on her other side and hardly able to get a word in, other than enthusiastic offers of condiments. The Bishop had already discovered that Frøken Frøystad was hoping to be ordained next year, and that Frøken Paulsen was already in fact the incumbent of a small parish in Western Norway. The Bishop was a committed supporter of the ordination of women, in so far as he could ever commit his magpie intellect to any one side of a question. He made sprightly fun of his opponents in the Anglican debates on the question.

'Of course the poor things are all Papists in spirit, without the guts to go the whole hog,' he ended up. 'In their heart of hearts they agree with Pope Paul that true women's liberation takes place over the cradle and the kitchen sink.'

'Certainly we in Norway have been surprised at how slowly things seem to have gone over here,' said Bente Frøystad.

'Never be surprised when things go slowly in Britain,' said the Bishop. 'We are the nation of the go-slow. And for every one with-it clergyman – ' he cast a significant, quick glance in the direction of Philip Lambton, and couldn't help drawing in his breath in a gesture of distaste – 'there are hundreds of neolithic monstrosities who have sleepless nights if they see a girl in shorts going round their

church, and compose fulminations on the subject for their
parish magazines. My goodness, the British Army is liberal-
minded and up-to-date compared to the outer reaches of
the Church of England !'

'That is very true,' said Philip Lambton from Frøken
Frøystad's other side; 'I could tell you some things about
the attitudes of my bishops . . .' And accordingly he did.
The Bishop of Peckham, having lost the initiative for the
moment, and having little curiosity about the misdeeds of
his fellow bishop, concentrated on his food : good plain
English fare, cooked by someone with a flair. It was solid
and satisfying, as a meal in a country hotel used often to
be before the war. If this was standard fare at St Botolph's,
then the Community certainly did themselves well. The
meal was served by brothers from the kitchen quarters,
quiet and nondescript; the portions were substantial, but
there were no second helpings (the Reverend Fleishman
established that). At the end of the meal, Father Anselm, at
the Bishop of Peckham's request, said a short grace, and
then they all withdrew to the little side room for coffee.

Here everybody began to relax considerably. It was a
relief not to be sitting in the shadow of the assembled
brothers. It occurred to Ernest Clayton that what was un-
nerving about them was that ordinary men – not Father
Anselm, of course, but middle-of-the-road men – seemed
to lose all individuality as soon as they got out of their
everyday clothes into the monks' habit. It was as if our
identity amounted to no more than the shade of a sports
jacket, the stripe of a tie. For most of the delegates the
unpleasant thing about sitting in the company of the
brothers was the suspicion that most of them were imagining future orgies of shocking proportions in the guest
quarters, thanks to the unprecedented female invasion of
the Community. Most of the delegates had little doubt that
a monk's imagination, when it got to work, would paint
reality in the most unlikely brilliant colours, due to his long
deprivation.

The fact that Father Anselm withdrew along with his flock also seemed to lighten the atmosphere. His air of un-breachable gravity was impressive, but hardly companion-able. Coffee was waiting for them in the side room, they served themselves and each other, and this helped to break any remaining ice. Then they settled down into cosy little groups. The Bishop of Mitabezi, wiser in his generation, this time secured Bente Frøystad, on the pretext of wishing to thank her for the sterling support of the Norwegian delegation at the recent World Council meeting (though he hadn't bothered to give thanks for this to Randi Paulsen) and also for the splendid work of the Norwegian missions throughout Central Africa (though in fact he had just heard about these for the first time from Frøken Paulsen). But the Bishop was not allowed to keep her to himself: he had to share her with Philip Lambton, Brother Dominic and Simeon P. Fleishman. The Bishop of Peckham sighed at the waste of Bente Frøystad on such inferior clerical material, but he submitted with Christian resignation and did his duty by Randi Paulsen, assisted by Ernest Clayton and the aggressive Stewart Phipps.

In the background hovered the other two brothers who had opted to attend the symposium, uneasy figures whom nobody could fit in, sometimes talking in a low voice to-gether, sometimes looking on at the groups and the dis-cussions with expressions of assumed blandness.

Discussions soon became animated, with a degree of friendly consultation between the groups. It soon emerged (as the Bishop of Peckham had already suspected) that each contributor had a quite different notion of what should be discussed in the coming days under the blanket heading of the Social Role of the Church in the Modern World. (Why on earth hadn't they been more specific at Church House, thought Peckham; another black mark, and won't I blow them up there.) The group around the Bishop of Mitabezi managed a degree of common ground: Simeon P. Fleishman's absorbing interest in fund-raising was shared

by the Bishop, and the uses to which the latter would put
them were of some interest to Bente Frøystad, whose main
concerns were the underdeveloped nations and sexual
politics. This left Philip Lambton and Brother Dominic
out in the cold, but the former could never be there long,
and he launched with naïve enthusiasm into an enthusiastic
monologue on religious motifs in recent top twenty hits.
Brother Dominic, his face a veritable mask, listened or did
not listen, glazed and glacial.

The other group was far less happy. Stewart Phipps
launched into an inevitable tirade about American colonial-
ism and multi-national corporations; the Bishop, goaded
by his itch for paradox, defended both, as he would have
defended Attila the Hun or the Marquis de Sade if they
had been attacked by Stewart Phipps. Randi Paulsen was
frankly bored by the discussion : the differences between
the political parties in her native country were so tiny that
politics had virtually ceased to exist for her long ago.
After a time she turned to Ernest Clayton and with a
sweet smile that said, 'We'll let the boys play their silly little
games, shall we?' she began to question him about Sunday
school attendance in his parish. Here again the discussion
was not entirely happy, for Ernest Clayton was honest
enough to admit to his belief that within fifty years
Christianity would be nothing more than a folk memory
in his part of Lincolnshire. Finding his attitude strange and
his answers unsatisfactory, Randi Paulsen decided that she
would go up and fetch some educational material from
her room.

'Because it is so sad,' she said, with a sweetly forgiving
smile on her face, 'to see the little ones growing up in such
a terrible darkness, just the very ones whom Our Lord
specially called to Him.'

There was nothing one could reply to this, but the Bishop,
scenting a new challenge, wrenched himself from a defence
of the CIA's role in the assassination of President Allende,
and, on her return bearing a pile of brightly coloured

literature, turned towards her with a deceptive courtesy and interest.

'Ah yes,' he said, 'this was something we were discussing this afternoon. Now what would be the figures for church attendance in Norway?'

'We have ninety per cent membership of the National Church among the population as a whole,' said Randi Paulsen complacently.

'But that wasn't quite what I asked, you see,' said the Bishop. 'I confess I have heard some such figure before, but it's a fiddle, is it not? The vicar does all the birth certificates, or some such wheeze, and you don't get one till the christening? But what I was asking about was the actual proportion who come to church.'

'It is somewhat lower,' admitted Randi Paulsen.

'How much lower?' said the Bishop, dropping his urbanity entirely.

'About eight per cent are church-goers,' said Randi reluctantly.

'Ah ha,' said the Bishop. 'We don't seem to hear that figure quite so often.'

'But we are making very big efforts with our young people,' said Randi, clambering back on to her hobby horse. 'In a lot of the country districts we have managed to stop the cinema shows and the Saturday dances –'

'*What?*' said Philip Lambton from the next table, unable to believe his ears that such nineteenth-century obscurantism should exist anywhere in the modern world, let alone Scandinavia.

'Yes, we're pleased about this,' said Randi Paulsen, 'because these were a great temptation, and the young people are now left completely open to us and our efforts. And of course we are not being entirely negative. We're producing some really excellent books and records on religious subjects, aimed specially at young people of all ages.'

She opened one of her books and beamed her dreadful smile around the room.

'I wish I could play you some of the records,' she said. 'Such pretty songs about Jesus. But this is just one of the books, and you'll see how lovely the illustrations are!'

She opened a large, colourful volume, which was clearly a version of the gospel story nearly digested out of existence and adapted to limited understanding and minimal vocabulary. As she spread the work out on her lap the first thing that met the Bishop's eye was a truly dreadful work of art, in manner influenced by the lowest common denominator of Victorian religiosity, in colour outvying the worst the pre-Raphaelite palate could perpetrate: a blond, Nordic Christ, looking like a benevolent young sailor, was gazing out over a Hollywood-green landscape, and was clearly about to launch into the Sermon on the Fjell. The Bishop of Peckham screwed up his mouth.

'That sort of thing strikes me as nothing more than religious pornography,' he said.

Randi Paulsen looked at him for a moment in disbelief. Then she snapped the book shut, and clasped her hands over her abdomen. She seemed about to say something very cutting to the Bishop, but her Norwegian respect for rank asserted itself in time, and she merely drew her lips thinly together. After a few moments of this silence the forgiving smile began to battle its way back on to her face. In time it won, but she nevertheless spent much of the rest of the evening in silence.

But she didn't manage to cast a blight over the rest of the company: the talk soon turned to salaries and stipends, and became general between the two groups as they all swapped poverty stories. Simeon P. Fleishman's brain became involved in a series of complicated conversions between the dollar and the pound, and when he came up with the answers his aghast looks at the miserable condition of his denominational English brethren were a source of great delight to Ernest Clayton. The discussions rather left Brother Dominic, who presumably had renounced money along with so much else, out in the cold, but the few attempts to draw him in met with such stiff responses that all gave up after a while and launched into further fanciful discussions of means of supplementing their incomes. It was cheering to note that this was a topic which Stewart Phipps joined in as enthusiastically as everyone else, with only the occasional glance at 'socio-economic structures' and the like. One touch of salary makes the whole world kin.

It was Father Anselm who broke up the party. The brothers had been in the chapel at their evening service. The Bishop had suggested that the delegates should give the service a miss that first evening, in order to get to know each other better, and the sound of the singing had made a pleasant background to their discussion of ways and means. 'How immensely spiritual,' Simeon Fleishman had said, interrupting his exposition of a knotty point of investment policy to listen for a couple of seconds. Shortly after the singing stopped Father Anselm appeared in the archway, surveyed the assembled delegates for a moment, as if to say 'how of the world, worldly', and then said : 'After compline we usually go straight to our cells. Perhaps you would care to do the same, after your hard day of travelling.'

It was a more impressive way of saying, 'Time, gentlemen, please.' They all got up, a little shamefaced, they knew not why. Father Anselm led the way through the low dark passages and up the stairs, his brown robe billowing out behind him. When they reached the guest wing, a broad, dim corridor with doors opening out from both sides, he merely said, 'Good night to you all,' inclined his head, and turned to go down the stairs again.

'One moment,' said the clear voice of Randi Paulsen. The voice, perhaps merely because it was female, seemed to affect Father Anselm unpleasantly. His shoulders stiffened. He turned to face her without speaking. 'There is no lock on the door to my room,' continued Randi, unabashed.

'That is correct. There are no locks on any of the doors,' Father Anselm answered.

Randi Paulsen, standing in the doorway of her room, gazed out of her window at the moors and the great barn, her lips compressed and her manner saying: 'There may be marauders waiting for me, inside or out.' Aloud she said: 'It is necessary for me to be able to lock my door and my window.'

Father Anselm, with a kind of dour patience, tried to explain: 'The decision to have no locks on the door was taken by the founder of St Botolph's. He believed that there was no time of day or night when the devil might not perplex the mind with doubts and difficulties of the spirit. We might put the idea rather differently today, but the argument remains valid and the situation does arise – particularly as we have the occasional visitor who is in retreat to wrestle with spiritual problems. In such cases there is sometimes a need for company, so that the doubts may be met with together and fought, or so that the prayer may be communal rather than solitary.'

He turned to go.

'That does not solve the problem,' said Randi Paulsen.

'It is not my problem,' said Father Anselm. 'The rule of the order is quite definite on this point.'

And he proceeded down the narrow stone steps.

'I've no doubt you will be perfectly safe,' said the Bishop of Peckham briskly. 'Let's to our beds.' But one glance at her pinched lips and militant stance convinced him that the problem was not to be solved by the cold water of common sense. 'Well, perhaps Miss Frøystad and you could sleep together, then.'

'That is quite unnecessary,' said Bente Frøystad in a thoroughly down-to-earth manner. 'The beds are small and I need a good night's sleep.' She made off with a no-nonsense walk in the direction of her room, and then, as a thought struck her, turned and pointed to a heavy wooden wardrobe by the wall of the corridor. 'Couldn't somebody push that into her room?'

And she went into her room and shut the door in a manner designed to suggest that anyone intending to take advantage of her in her sleep would do well to think again. The rest looked at each other, while Randi Paulsen waited.

'That's a job for you young ones,' said the Bishop of Peckham. 'Good night to you all.'

So, puffing and blowing, Stewart Phipps and Philip Lambton, aided by some bulky shoves from Simeon Fleishman, pushed the wardrobe into Randi Paulsen's room, and left it by the door. They were rewarded by a frosty nod. Randi Paulsen's room was at the rear end of the corridor, by the stair-head and the lavatory, and those who availed themselves of the latter facility heard heavy shunting sounds as the heavy piece was pushed into position by Frøken Paulsen herself. There were sounds of flushing and running water, and the odd call from the birds on the moor outside. Then night reigned over the Community of St Botolph's. It was the first time in its existence that women had been inside the walls, but no signs were vouchsafed of the wrath of the heavens. Most of its inhabitants slept quite soundly.

CHAPTER IV

CONFERRING

THE SYMPOSIUM got off to a reasonably good start. Early communion was followed by a simple breakfast of brown bread, cheese and milk, and though it wasn't what they were used to (particularly the Bishop, who was quite Edwardian in his love of a heavy and varied breakfast), it made them all feel healthy and holy – at peace with the world, and even fairly well disposed towards each other.

The setting for the discussions was a moderate-sized room near to Father Anselm's office, reached down the same dark corridor. But unlike the office, which was dark and windowless, the conference room turned out to be light and airy, and to have a good view of the kitchen gardens around the main buildings and of the Community's wall, stretching into the distance. The occasional sheep even presented itself for inspection, giving more than one of the participants (particularly the urban-based ones) a feeling that 'this was what Christianity was all about', though they would have been hard put to it to explain precisely what they meant by that. Inside the room was a long, heavy table, for use if the discussion was of a large or formal character. But this was rarely the case at St Botolph's, which liked to keep its gatherings small and intimate, so in the other part of the room there was a collection of comparatively easy chairs. It was at this end that the various delegates settled themselves.

If the principal delegates had loosened up considerably by the time the proceedings began, there was little change to be observed in the three brothers who sat in on the discussions, nor, indeed, in Father Anselm. They, of course, were on home territory, and it was natural that the first impressions they made should need less modification than for those who were among strangers, in a strange place. It was symptomatic that Brother Dominic brought upright chairs over from the table, clearly implying that he had no intention of indulging his spine. The three sat together, a little apart, Brother Dominic occasionally leaning over and talking in a low voice to the elderly, snuffed-out one, presumably interpreting what was being said. Was he deaf, Ernest Clayton wondered? And were there no brothers with unimpaired hearing who might have liked to attend, and might have been able to contribute more?

Father Anselm did take an easy chair, but it took more than comfort to make him unbend. His fearsome gravity hung over him still, like a cloud, and the air of chilling disapproval which had been evident from the arrival of the Norwegian delegation was with him still. The chief nourisher of life's feast certainly didn't seem to have knitted up his ravell'd sleave of care.

When the Bishop of Peckham introduced the proceedings with his little speech – cunningly delivered as if it were a complete improvisation – about how paradoxical that a symposium on the role of the Church in the modern world should meet in a community which had withdrawn itself from the world, he threw a friendly, join-the-circle glance in Father Anselm's direction, and seemed about to address further remarks directly at him. He received in return a momentary widening of the mouth, which showed a few shadowy teeth behind the brown beard, but which could hardly be called the wintriest of smiles. The eyes remained iced over. The Bishop seemed to think again. From then on, Father Anselm took no part in the session, and no one had the temerity to try to draw him in.

In the course of the initial discussion, the various delegates began to reveal more of themselves, to get beyond their own little obsessions and show the disinterested observer what they were made of. Philip Lambton, for example, though his topic was inevitably youth and the gulf between the Church and the rising generation, took a wide view of the subject, and found some things to say that were very superior to his fatuities of the night before. He gave the impression that he might have been a useful minister of the Church if he had not been seduced by the glamour and glitter of clerical show-biz. In reply to his call for the Church to re-examine its message, Ernest Clayton put in a note of mild dissent.

'Re-examine our message, of course, in the light of the facts of the modern world. But I sometimes think we re-examine our message in the light of every stray breeze of opinion from the popular press, and every fashionable aberration in taste and behaviour. One wonders in the long run whether it would not be better for the Church to stand – as it so often has had to in the past – changeless in the midst of change. People might come back to such a church. I doubt if they ever will to a church that is always puffing along to catch the bus five minutes after the bus has gone.'

Simeon Fleishman had little to say, and that little was embarrassing. Luckily he limited his main contribution that first morning to endorsing a plea for unity and fellow-ship among Christians of all kinds put out by Randi Paulsen. She seemed to have caught up with the ecumenical movement five minutes after that bus had gone – perhaps because of an invincible distrust of the Roman Catholic Church, which growled along in an undertone during the early part of her speech. She sounded like Margaret Thatcher wooing the Trade Unions. That was, in fact, the most interesting thing about her speech, which was as a whole singularly lacking in intellectual grasp, let alone originality.

'After all,' she concluded, 'we are all united in our belief in the divinity of the Lord Jesus.'

She sprinkled her Christian charity in the form of a tight-lipped smile around the other delegates, but she seemed disconcerted on hearing throat-rumblings of dissent from the Bishop of Peckham.

'Should we lay too much stress on that, do you think?' he said with a puckish glance at the rest.

'At least, then,' said Randi firmly, 'we are united in a belief in God.'

'Ah,' said the Bishop, leaning back, 'but what do we mean by the term God?'

Ernest Clayton found himself wondering about the Bishop. Obviously he had a little act all his own, which he was immensely pleased with. Equally obviously, one of the things he enjoyed doing was setting the cat among the pigeons. On the other hand, Clayton sensed somewhere a soft centre, a personal rather than an intellectual flabbiness, as if he were someone it would not do to rely on if things came to the crunch.

At least the Bishop kept control of his sense of humour sufficiently to ensure a considerable degree of harmony until lunch. By then it had suggested itself to Ernest Clayton that there was some method in his tactics, for Randi Paulsen avoided him like the plague as the delegates drifted towards the great hall, and he therefore secured Bente Frøystad as his seating partner, the Bishop of Mitabezi getting landed once more with the unappealing Randi (it was clear, at least to them, that the ladies were the property – or at least were under the protection – of the bishops, and none of the rest had the guts to dispute their assumption of an episcopal *droit de seigneur*).

After lunch it had been agreed that an hour or so should be set aside for relaxation or for walking off the meal. The Bishop of Peckham went up to his room, whence were shortly heard loud and determined snores. Among the rest, groups and alliances seemed in the process of forming. Randi Paulsen had decided that Philip Lambton was the only member of the group with whom she could feel any sympathy at all – and that not much; accordingly she commandeered him in her limpet way, and they went off for a stroll on to the moorland which lay within the Community wall. As they passed Ernest Clayton in the kitchen garden, he heard Randi say : 'It seems to me so terribly sad that a bishop of the Church should apparently spend so much of his time spreading doubt about the gospel message.'

'You should hear my bishop on the subject of Peckham,' replied Philip Lambton boyishly. 'Won't hear a word in his favour. Not that he's any better himself, of course – completely out of touch . . .'

Their voices faded from Clayton's hearing as they came to the heather and strode manfully out.

Both bishops, in fact, had graciously surrendered their rights to the ladies and left second nibble to others. Bente Frøystad had been secured by Stewart Phipps, and they made a striking couple walking up and down the lawn near the outer gate – she, firmly-made and well-shaped, a strong, healthy figure; he thin, tall, hardly able to contain his energy which seemed to result in a certain degree of ill-co-ordination. They were giving the woman question a belated thrashing.

'If only my wife thought like you,' Clayton heard Phipps say in his nervous, intense, rather unpleasant voice. 'We've gone into the question over and over again, but she's terribly lukewarm.'

Stewart Phipps had a meek little drudge of a wife in his council house home, who spent her days washing nappies and trying to bring together ends that would not meet. When the woman question could be ignored no longer (he had initially condemned it as a typical diversionary tactic on the part of the ruling cadre to divert attention from the working-class struggle) Stewart Phipps had bullied his wife into attending meetings and forming parties on the subject, and had even offered to take care of the children now and then while she did so, but she had little heart for the struggle, the leadership went to others, and Phipps had (not too regretfully) let the matter lapse.

The Bishop of Mitabezi, meanwhile, had managed to persuade Father Anselm out of his dark corridors and into the fresh air. The two of them – both, in different ways, commanding figures – went on an inspection tour of the Community's farming activities, examining the great barn and some of the hen runs, Father Anselm pointing out the finer features of various breeds of sheep. Finally they made for the pig sty, which was situated well away from the main building. Throughout the tour the Bishop seemed genuinely rather than nominally absorbed in the subject, looked closely at the hens and sheep, asked detailed questions, and poked and pried into odd corners of the barn and chicken run, his eyes aglow with interest.

That left Simeon P. Fleishman. For some time Ernest Clayton feared he was going to get landed with him, but passing in his wanderings down one side of the Great Hall he came across an unexpected window (when one was inside, the large windows at the far end so dominated that one didn't notice any others). This one was a musty little affair, hidden in a recess, but through it he saw Simeon P., alone in the hall, picking up and examining the silver goblets and chalices on the heavy oak dresser beside the high table. Ernest Clayton smiled wryly, and continued his wanderings around the gardens. Some time later he glimpsed Fleishman, sitting on one of the rare seats over near the lawn, his jacket off (but folded neatly beside him), his sleeves rolled up, writing away busily at something or other, using one leg crooked over the other as a writing desk. Probably a letter to his congregation, thought Clayton; something for the parish magazine as a return for his travel expenses.

So Clayton wandered, and relaxed, and noticed things, in the hot summer air. The farm buildings, which he visited after the Bishop and Father Anselm had left, were commodious and clean – almost fastidiously so. It was almost as if they were playing at farming. Though perhaps there

were so many of them, and they had so much time, that it
was not surprising that they could keep things in the sort
of state that no ordinary farmer would aspire to.

There were no brothers occupied in agricultural labour
at that moment, however. One or two were to be seen out
on the moors – Old Testament figures, with the wind
blowing their robes. Some were walking around the main
building, singly or in pairs, the latter sometimes talking in
low voices. None of them spoke to Clayton.

At one point in his walk he caught a sidelong glimpse
of a brother, kicking his heels (if the expression is not too
secular) by the corner of the big barn. Something in his
stance reminded the Reverend Clayton of someone he had
seen – someone he had known? One of his parishioners,
perhaps? Surely not. He would certainly have heard if one
of them had done such an unlikely thing as take himself
off to a monastery. And indifference reigned so supreme in
Ashfield that it was difficult enough getting anyone to come
to church, let alone engage in any more strenuous spiritual
exercise. Ernest Clayton frowned. Who could it be – or
was it just an optical illusion?

But when he looked again, the brother was gone.

By dinner time the delegates had divided themselves into
two friendly, or fairly friendly groups, easily discernible to
any eye skilled in observing the herd instincts of humanity
suddenly thrust as strangers together. One group consisted
of the vaguely radically-orientated, collecting themselves
around the Bishop of Peckham – Bente Frøystad, Stewart
Phipps and Ernest Clayton (not because he thought of himself as particularly radical, but because the smiles of peace
and goodwill to all men which Randi Paulsen dispensed
like nourishing soup all around her group made him want
to throw up). Tagging along vaguely with this group was
Brother Dominic, though Clayton thought this was for
reasons similar to his own : he seemed particularly to avoid
Randi Paulsen, especially in company, though he had seen

them exchange a few words in one of the dark corridors behind the main hall as Randi came down the stairs for breakfast.

Around the Bishop of Mitabezi, and much occupied with the supply of mealies and missionaries to the underdeveloped countries, were Randi herself, Philip Lambton and Simeon Fleishman (for no reason of interest or affection, but because he classed the Bishop's circle as radical – 'dangerously radical' in fact, for the two words always went together in the mid-Western city where he dispensed non-denominational doctrine – and because he was fed up with Stewart Phipps's insistence on putting him in the dock and subjecting him to a bully-ragging inquisition). To this group attached themselves the middle-aged and the elderly brothers, and the two of them looked on, silent and uneasy.

Their names, at least, the Bishop of Mitabezi managed to worm out of them. The middle-aged one was Brother Hamish, and the elderly one was Brother Jonathan. The latter still seemed as close to extinction as one could well be without having the fact entered at Somerset House. Yet once or twice he fluttered his hands to his face, and seemed about to make a gesture of protest which never materialized, and may in fact have been something quite different – a bad migraine, for example. Brother Hamish – watery-eyed, even shifty, with unhealthy-looking, sparse hair and a dingy complexion – seemed to be following Brother Dominic's lead in helping Brother Jonathan to understand the conversation. He was rewarded by an occasional word thrown his way by Randi Paulsen – to which he replied with nervous half-smiles or monosyllables.

Eventually the talk became more general, and less business-like. The Bishop of Peckham, perhaps trying to account in his own mind for the singularly ill-assorted nature of the group, started the chat in the direction of 'how they had all come to be there'. Simeon Fleishman was very ready with his explanation.

'Waall,' he said, tilting himself forward the better to

ooze sincerity, 'I'm on a visit to your wonderful country
to study trends in church-design. This is a kind of sabbatical
financed by my parishioners in consequence of the fact
that we plan to erect an entirely new structure in the fore-
seeable future, inflation in building costs permitting. So
I've been around to Coventry, Liverpool – ' My God, how
big is his new structure going to be? thought Ernest Clayton – 'and I had a very stimulating exchange of perspectives
with the Bishop of Barstowe when I visited there a few
weeks ago. In fact, he raised the contingency of me coming
here, which I truly am grateful to him for, because it sure
is proving a truly spiritually stimulating experience.'

Barstowe, thought the Bishop of Peckham. Of course he
knew I would be here. Inflicting bores on me in sheer
malice. For the Bishop was not loved by his fellow bishops,
and he knew it.

Bente Frøystad explained: 'We have this feeling in
Norway that women have been excluded and under-repre-
sented for so long on committees, official bodies and so on
that it is time to tilt the balance a little in the other
direction.'

'Very commendable,' said the Bishop.

'Also,' continued Bente Frøystad, smiling, 'educated
Norwegians tend to be a little shy about speaking English
in front of each other – it is a sort of status symbol – and as
we had both been au pair girls here, and were fairly confident, they decided we might be able to play our parts
better than any of the men.'

'Au pairs, eh?' said the Bishop eagerly. 'Now how did
you find that experience?'

'Slave labour,' said Bente Frøystad.

'Of course one could be lucky,' said Randi Paulsen. Her
hands fluttered nervously to her hair, and her eyes, blinking,
went down into her lap. 'But I have heard of several girls
who have had some *most* unpleasant experiences!'

No one enquired further, and the pursed lips did not
encourage them to.

'It's a sad thing,' said Ernest Clayton. 'The au pair system could be such a good one for all parties, and yet it seems to work out either as a scandal or a joke.'

'I don't see anything good in the privileged classes getting cheap labour,' said Stewart Phipps.

'Does your wife go out to work?' enquired Bente Frøystad.

'No, of course not,' said Phipps.

'Then you merely married your au pair,' said Bente. The alliance seemed to have become more fragile since the afternoon walk. The male sympathizer with women's lib is in roughly the same position as the white liberal in the American racial conflict, and gets about as much thanks.

Randi Paulsen seemed to want to turn the conversation back to her own experiences. 'The stories I could tell about things that have happened to Norwegian girls in England are quite appalling,' she said with a twisted expression on her face. 'You wouldn't believe it possible.'

She left the phrase suspended in the air, perhaps hoping that someone would press her. But they all seemed to prefer to stick to the general rather than the particular.

'Of course we have the idea that Scandinavian girls all know how to look after themselves,' said the Bishop. 'But is this always the case? I seem to remember reading statistics that suggest the proportion of girls already pregnant when they marry is very high.'

'Quite untrue,' snapped Randi Paulsen.

'True enough,' said Bente Frøystad. 'But we prefer to choose the man we're pregnant by.' This remark earned her a furious look from Randi, who looked as if she was treasuring up such remarks to report them back to the Church authorities.

It was unnecessary to ask how the others had got there: they had been recommended by their bishops – because they needed a rest, needed feeding up, or needed to get away from their wives. Those, at any rate, were the usual

reasons. The Bishop of Mitabezi had been recommended
to come by Church House, to keep him out of their hair,
and to ensure that he didn't make too many fiery statements
to the press. Some organs were still pretty unhappy about
Christian Socialism, and most certainly drew the line at
Christian terrorism.

Ernest Clayton was about to take the conversation a
stage further by enquiring anew into the topic he had
raised on the first night – why the brothers had decided to
take orders, what background they came from, and what
were their experiences outside the walls that made them
take their decisions – when he looked in the direction of
Brother Dominic. His face, usually set, though not serene,
was now apparently in the grip of some strong emotion or
other. His strong will seemed to be getting the upper hand,
but the ugly force of the passion inside him was impossible
to hide altogether. At that moment Brother Dominic looked
very unpleasant indeed.

Ernest Clayton changed his mind about bringing up that
particular subject. 'I'm for my bed,' he said. 'I'm an early
bird at home, if only to save electricity.'

His move gave a general signal to break up. The three
brothers evaporated quietly, without fuss. With the rest,
rather more pother was created and more formality observed, but eventually they made their way tentatively up
their dark staircase – Father Anselm had not been seen
since the evening meal, and the light switches were difficult
to find – and into their rooms. Again, noises of ablution
and evacuation were dimly audible through the thick stone
walls, as was the determined sound of Randi Paulsen
dragging her wardrobe across her door. Then all that was
to be heard, and that only if one put one's ear close to the
door, were the snores of My Lord of Peckham.

The snores continued intermittently for some hours. The
Bishop liked his sleep. But at half past two in the morning,
when – half asleep – he was leaning over to his little shelf

to get a drink of water, he thought he heard a sound. Shaking the sleep from his head, he took a gulp of water. Then the noise came again, more insistently.

Someone was knocking at his door.

'Come in,' he said, feeling rather ridiculous, and if the truth were known, rather scared.

CHAPTER V

'THE VOICE OF THY BROTHER'S BLOOD'

THE DOOR SWUNG open, and through the darkness the Bishop of Peckham perceived a shape entering the room quietly. It was all so like a Gothic horror novel that in the normal way the Bishop's sense of humour would have delighted in the situation. The trouble was that, at the moment, he felt like doing nothing so much as making the classic response to such situations – pulling the blanket over his head and shrieking to the thing to go away. Especially when it turned round, slowly and shut the door.

'Who are you?' said the Bishop, all too aware of the quaver in his voice. 'What do you want?'

'Father Anselm,' said the shape, pausing at the foot of the bed. 'Please get up and put on your clothes.'

The command put a grain of fighting-spirit back into the Bishop. He had never liked being told what to do, even in the Second World War, in which he had served, wittily.

'Look here,' he protested, 'this is thoroughly reprehensible. Coming here in the dead of night, scar . . . when you might have scared me to death – and throwing out orders in that way. I mean, anyone would think we were behind the Iron Curtain!'

'You must be considered leader of this symposium,' said Father Anselm, not moving from his minatory position at the foot of the bed. 'I have to consult you before I do anything. I must ask you to do as I suggested at once.'

The Bishop was surprisingly easily cowed. Father Anselm had the sort of rock-steady assurance that his ironies could not dent. And, besides, looking at the black outline, unmoving and unmoved, gazing at him across the expanse of bed, he found that his teeth still displayed a disconcerting desire to chatter. He got up, turned on the little bed-light on his shelf, and then pulled on his socks and shoes, and put on the smart Austin Reed dressing-gown hanging by a hook near his bed. He groped and fumbled, for his equanimity was still far from restored.

'Well,' he said at last, squaring his shoulders, 'I'm ready. Though I can't for the life of me ...'

Father Anselm said nothing, but turned abruptly with a swirl of his habit, and led the way through the door. The dim light over the staircase was on, but not that in the corridor. They therefore aimed themselves in that direction, Father Anselm as usual keeping the upper hand by being much more confident in his movements than the Bishop. Though the Bishop felt better as soon as he made the stair-well, still he was disconcerted to realize that his heart was beating very hard indeed. It was almost as if he was expecting to find some ecclesiastical secret policeman at the end of their quest, who would put him through a series of inquisitions, with rack and strappado, on the subject of his various heresies.

They came to the cloister around the main hall, where one or two lights had been switched on, casting little light, but immense shadows. They plunged down the dark corridor leading to Father Anselm's office, but they did not stop there. They went instead further along, past one door, and then stopped by a second. Father Anselm paused, and turned towards the Bishop.

'Prepare yourself,' he said grimly.

The Bishop's heart, which had been doing a hectic tribal dance, suddenly seemed to stop altogether. The situation seemed to call upon him to say something, but though he swallowed, he could force nothing out. At last he managed a very feeble little nod.

Father Anselm, quietly and carefully, pushed down the mock-medieval door-handle, and swung open the door. It did not squeak, or possibly the Bishop would have sunk, a jibbering mass of terror, to the floor. As it was, he could

scarcely summon up the nerve to force one foot in front
of the other.

The room was lighted by the same sort of little bedside-
lamp as was in his room. Father Anselm having swirled
into the room, the Bishop stood in the doorway, blinking
to accustom his eyes to the lurking shadows. After a few
seconds he got his bearings and saw.

'Goodness me,' said the Bishop of Peckham.

It was one of his favourite expressions, but it could not
be considered adequate to this occasion. On the bed lay
Brother Dominic, clad in a rough white bed-robe. At least,
it had been white. Now the whole of the middle part of it
was savagely cut to ribbons, and heavy with thick red blood,
which had spurted over the walls and dripped in sticky
pools on to the floor. It looked as if a manic gorilla had
been at him with a knife and ripped his bowels out.

There was, needless to say, no sign of life. Brother
Dominic was presumably, at this very moment, freezing his
Lord.

The Bishop, having seen much, much more than he
wanted to, turned aside from the sight, leaned his head
against the door-post and retched. Nothing much came up,
but he heaved and heaved and heaved again, like a dog
who has eaten something he had better have left alone
(though dinner had, in fact, been good). Before long he felt
a hand on his shoulder, and let himself be led along the
corridor to Father Anselm's study.

The very closing of the door brought relief to the
Bishop's mind. The Thing was shut out. The Sight was not
before his eyes. The Bishop sank into a chair, wishing his
stomach was not still suggesting he was on the North Sea.
The voice of Father Anselm seemed to come from a great
distance.

'Now,' he said, 'the point is, what are we to do?'

The Bishop, trying desperately to concentrate on what
was going on, asked him to repeat what he had said.

'The question is,' repeated Anselm carefully, looking

straight at the Bishop, 'what we are to do.'

The Bishop shook his head violently, as if ridding him-self of the last vestiges of sleep and nausea.

'You've called the police?' he said at last.

'Not yet,' said Father Anselm quietly. 'I thought I should have your authorization.' The Bishop seemed about to say something, and Father Anselm added : 'Because this thing will inevitably come back to one of the members of your symposium.'

There was a pause.

'How is that?' asked the Bishop finally.

'The other members of the Community, the Brothers, sleep in the East Wing. The door between it and the main building is locked every night. We have some valuable silver in the main hall and some priceless things in the chapel. Since it would be child's play for a thief to get over the outer walls, it is necessary to minimize the number of possible means of entry. In practice, the only way into the Great Hall is through the door you came in when you arrived. The chapel has no entrance to the outside world – you remember it is reached by a small passage, the door to which is at the end of this corridor. This central block is entirely shut off from the rest of the Community's build-ings at night.'

'I see,' said the Bishop faintly.

'The main door is, of course, locked and bolted from the inside at night,' pursued Father Anselm remorselessly. 'Brother Dominic is – was – my assistant and personal servant. Only he and I sleep in this part of the building as a general rule. And then, of course, there are the guest-rooms . . .'

There was silence for a moment.

'I see,' said the Bishop. 'So he must have been killed either by you, or by one of us.'

'As far as the police are concerned, that is so,' said Father Anselm austerely. 'As far as *I* am concerned, he must have been killed by one of you.'

'Quite, quite,' said the Bishop feebly. He made a heroic effort to collect his thoughts. 'But of course you must in any case ring the police,' he said finally, gesturing in the direction of the discreet telephone in the murkiest corner of the room.

Father Anselm's mouth tightened. 'Very well,' he said. 'Now I have your permission.' He rose, and was proceeding in the direction of the telephone when both men were arrested by a sound.

The Bishop sat bolt upright and felt a tingling in his scalp which made him wonder if his hair was about to stand on end. It had been, to be sure, a very slight sound, and it seemed to have come from a long way off, penetrating the substantial door of Father Anselm's study. But it was a sound which unmistakably suggested a human being, and presumably one somewhere in the central block. The Bishop's look showed what he undeniably felt – that he had already had as much as, or more than, a human being could take. He was to feel that several times more in the course of the night.

Father Anselm, too, had been riveted to the floor by the sound. His deep, unfathomable eyes stared into the distance. Then he said : 'There's someone out there. It sounded like the main door. But that's impossible.'

Noiselessly he turned towards the door of his room.

'Come with me,' he said to the Bishop.

'But don't you think – ' the Bishop began. But Father Anselm had swirled out of the room, and a second's meditation convinced the Bishop that the prospect of staying there alone, even with a door between him and whatever it was, was infinitely more terrifying than the prospect of following. He showed remarkable nimbleness in pattering out after his masterful host, whose undulating outline he perceived at the end of the dark corridor leading to the Great Hall. He started after it, but then he saw it stop suddenly. Involuntarily he stopped too, then, slowly and reluctantly, he made his way towards him, and finally stood shoulder to shoulder with him at the point where the corridor opened out into the Great Hall.

The sight that met their eyes was a horrifying one.

The main door had been swung open, and framed in the wash of moonlight stood the Bishop of Mitabezi. He too was wearing a white robe – though his was of African cut and style, and of richer material. He too was terrifyingly stained with red, one long splurge reaching from waist to toe.

He was standing there, in heaven's spotlight, gazing crazily ahead of him. The whites of his eyes seemed to pierce across the expanse of the Great Hall towards them, though his eyes were rolling. His bearing was that of a powerful man, but slouching, and with his hands outspread in a generous gesture, like a tenor finishing an aria with a sob and soliciting applause. But the tenor's hands would not be red. His were, both of them, very red indeed. They had stained the door-handle, and even as Father Anselm and the Bishop looked, their sticky coating began to drip down to the floor of the hall.

And then, to crown the ghastly horror of the scene, the Bishop of Mitabezi opened his mouth and began to croon a strange, low, atonal chant, which whispered its way round the Romanesque expanse of the Great Hall, and sent a fresh chill straight to the hearts of the two hearers, watching in the shadows at the far end.

CHAPTER VI

THE DAWN COMES UP LIKE THUNDER

IT WAS FATHER Anselm, inevitably, who took charge of the situation. Showing a degree of nerve surprising even for him, he tore his feet from the spot to which they seemed to have become rooted the moment the sight had come upon him and went across the great expanse of hall floor towards the hideous chanting figure.

The Bishop of Mitabezi continuing to advance into the Great Hall, showed no awareness of any other person in the vicinity. His eyes continued to roll alarmingly, his mouth, barely open and barely moving, continued to emit weird sounds, and from its corners began to dribble two little streams of saliva. Father Anselm was tense with anticipation – a fact that could be felt by the Bishop of Peckham yards away, even though his body was concealed by his billowing robe. He took a step towards the chanting figure, stretched out his arm, and touched his. As he did so, the Bishop of Peckham's heart leapt into his mouth, and the thought of some fearsome affray, with murderous figures in clerical robes struggling for their lives on the floor, and him expected to intervene – and would he dare to intervene? – came upon him with all the welcomeness of a thunderclap on a picnic party.

But no such affray succeeded. The Bishop of Mitabezi, still chanting, allowed himself to be led, still seeming quite unconscious of any other presence, across the Great Hall towards the corridor and stairs which led to the guest bedrooms. As the two figures merged into the gloom, the Bishop of Mitabezi's chant was beginning to fade into silence. The other bishop, watching in the shadows, had a sinking feeling that he ought to follow. Every brotherly feeling prompted him to give what help he could to Father Anselm in his difficult and highly unpleasant task. But he stayed where he was. Brotherly feelings were all very well, but they tended to evaporate with the remembrance of that body on the bed, and the gashes through the white robe, and the great splashes of red disfiguring it.

After what seemed like an eternity – and his experiences at St Botolph's were giving him a new and more vivid conception of the meaning of the word – he heard from the distance the shuffle of a foot, the creak of a stair, sounds of human movement. The horrible thought flashed through his brain that the moving human might be the Bishop of Mitabezi – that he had slaughtered Father Anselm, and was now athirst for more clerical blood. But when the figure finally appeared at the other side of the hall, its robes were dark. In his ecstasy of relief, the Bishop felt that some tribute was called for.

'Superb,' he whispered to the approaching figure, his gratitude giving his voice real sincerity. 'Quite incredibly brave.'

The muscles around Father Anselm's mouth tightened – could it be with contempt? – and he led the way back down the corridor into his own office. Once inside, with the door shut, the Bishop felt once more that feeling of welcome security gained, that sense of discovering at last a firm foothold after a long walk over ice. In spite of what he suspected to be Father Anselm's attitude towards his recent behaviour he felt he had to give voice once again to his appreciation. By emphasizing Father Anselm's quite exceptional bravery, he felt he established himself as a man of normal courage, rather than the abject coward he might otherwise seem.

'You have nerves of steel, my word you have!' he said.

'He gave no trouble,' murmured Father Anselm. 'He got straight into bed like a child, and went to sleep.'

A very nasty thought occurred to the Bishop.

'But there are no locks on his door,' he said in consternation. 'He could – '

'I *tied* him in bed,' said Father Anselm levelly. 'With the sheets.'

'Good gracious,' said the Bishop. '*What* a clever plan.'

Father Anselm, however, seemed oblivious of his flatteries, and his mind had gone back to the subject of what the Bishop of Mitabezi had already done, rather than what he might be feared to be about to do.

'A most extraordinary reversion,' he said, sitting down as stiffly as ever in the chair behind his desk. 'I suppose the early Church had experience of that kind of thing.'

'Certainly, certainly,' said the Bishop, allowing his thoughts to graze on the larger historical pastures, instead of centring on the hideously restricted grounds of the last half-hour or so. 'A common enough phenomenon, as the records show, not just here, but throughout Europe. Quite understandable, of course.'

'One wishes, in that case, that the Church authorities had shown themselves a little more aware of the dangers,' said Father Anselm with more than a touch of asperity. 'I have lost my most capable assistant and my probable successor!'

Again the memory of the body in the next room flooded over the Bishop, and he could only murmur, 'Quite, quite.'

'The consequences of all this are frightening to contemplate,' continued Father Anselm. 'But that, of course, will be your department rather than mine.'

'Consequences?' said the Bishop, nervous again.

'Clearly there will be publicity of the most damaging kind.' The Bishop flinched. 'And the effects in the Third World are anybody's guess.'

The words had a magic effect on the Bishop.

'The Third World! Oh, my goodness, yes! What do you think they'll say?'

'No doubt that this is all some capitalist-imperialist plot

to discredit the black races,' said Father Anselm. 'I expect you know the sort of thing better than I. And then of course the diplomatic repercussions will be endless.'

'My goodness,' said the Bishop, 'you alarm me. Church House will be livid. They were particularly insistent that I should keep him happy.'

'I doubt whether they intended you should go so far as to provide him with human sacrifices,' said Father Anselm.

'No, no, naturally,' said the Bishop. 'Nevertheless, they will be *most* upset. The one thing they are anxious to avoid at the moment is upsetting the Third World.' He paused for a moment. 'If only there were something that could be done . . .'

His voice faded into thoughtful silence.

Father Anselm looked at him hard. 'Are you suggesting that the whole thing be concealed?' he asked, in a soft voice which had no note of disapproval in it.

'No, no, of course not,' said the Bishop, but rather feebly. 'I'm merely going through the possibilities in my mind, naturally. In any case, the young man will have had relatives . . .'

'He had none,' said Father Anselm, in that same soft voice. 'He was quite alone when he came here. He told me so many times.'

The Bishop became lost in reverie. He loved publicity, fuss, people talking about him; he hated ridicule, being in the wrong, being put up against the wall. In his heart of hearts he would have liked to be the next Archbishop of Canterbury, though he sometimes doubted whether the Prime Minister was the man to make such an imaginative gesture. So circumspect had he been that he was sure nobody in the world knew of this secret ambition, but in fact one of the stalest jokes of the clerical circuit was that he was preparing himself for the job by being a very arch bishop indeed. Who could imagine an Archbishop of Canterbury who had recently (for the Bishop, being an optimist, always imagined the See of Canterbury being *shortly* vacant again, by one means or another) been involved in a murder case? It would be disastrous for the image. To put the matter at its lowest, how many television producers would be knocking at the palace door in the near future?

As the temptations of this unorthodox course of conduct became more pressing, the implications fanned out in his mind : he saw himself and Father Anselm digging a shallow grave on the moors, carrying out the . . . the Thing . . . and burying it, hugger-mugger. Would one of them say the burial service? He thought of all the evasions and concealments that would be necessary afterwards, the sessions of the symposium to be gone through as if nothing had happened. He thought of living with the memory, with the possibility of blackmail. All these considerations, which together might almost be said to add up to the promptings of a moral sense, crowded in on the Bishop. Suddenly he shook his head violently, got a grip on himself, and turned back to Father Anselm.

'Of course, the idea's absurd,' he said, 'quite absurd. You must ring the police at once.'

Father Anselm looked at him for a moment, then rose and again moved towards the telephone. His silence made the Bishop nervous once more.

'I presume your local police can be discreet,' he said.

'I have no experience of our local police,' said Father Anselm. All his former austerity of manner had now re-turned. He paused a second over the phone, almost as if to give the Bishop one last chance of changing his mind, then he lifted the receiver and dialled.

'Hickley Police Station? Good. I'm speaking from the Community of St Botolph's. My name is Father Anselm . . . That's right, I am. Now look, there has been a murder here . . . No, not an intruder, a murder . . . One of the brothers . . . If you would . . . And when you get here, please do not ring the bell. There's no reason to disturb the Community before it is necessary. I myself will wait for you in the grounds . . . Thank you – yes, if you would.'

He put the phone down, and came to the middle of the room. 'They are coming immediately,' he said coldly. 'I shall wait for them by the gate.'

'I'll wait with you,' said the Bishop with transparent eagerness.

As they walked across the floor of the Great Hall the Bishop averted his eyes from the drops of blood which had fallen from the Bishop of Mitabezi's hands, and stood aside while Father Anselm pushed open the door (which had swung to) without touching the handle. Once outside the Bishop took a deep breath of fresh air and looked around him. Birds were singing, it was beginning to get light. Another day was dawning for the brothers of the Community of St Botolph's. Or for all but one of them.

The before-dawn air was chill, and the Bishop shivered. Father Anselm was not proceeding in the direction of the gate, but was standing quite still. The Bishop, finding that erect, silent figure as awesome as ever, began rather nervously to make conversation.

'There is one blessing to be counted,' he said. 'The publicity will be ghastly, of course – quite ghastly – but at least there can be no doubt who did it, so it should all be over in the minimum possible time. That we can be grateful for. Whether we can keep the symposium going is another matter . . .'

But as he was talking he realized that Father Anselm was not listening. The spiritual leader of St Botolph's was peering through the half-light at a series of dreadful red patches on the ground. They seemed to come from the barn, and they got smaller and smaller, and less frequent as they came nearer the door into the Great Hall. Through the light of near-day could dimly be discerned a crude daubing of red on the side of the barn. The Bishop did not want to look: it all brought back too vividly the un-nerving events of the last two hours. He found it distasteful, in fact, that Father Anselm should seem so interested. Eventually the latter spoke.

'That's very odd,' he said. 'I don't understand it.'

'What?'

'They all seem to be coming the one way.'

The Bishop dragged his head round, and looked again at the trail of blood.

'What do you mean?'

'There was no blood in the Hall except what we saw drip from his hands,' said Father Anselm. He turned around and looked at the door-handle. It was very red, and sticky. 'There is blood on the *outside* door-handle, but none on the inside. And all this blood out here seems to be coming *from* the barn.'

Suddenly he seemed to make a decision, and impelled his body into action. He strode towards the barn, and the Bishop, after a moment of irritated hesitation, padded after him. They followed the trail of red, and paused briefly by the daubed sign on the near side wall of the barn : it looked like a crude and lop-sided version of the Cross of Lorraine. There was more blood on the ground in front of the barn. Father Anselm walked ahead resolutely. At the corner of the barn he stopped.

The Bishop of Peckham, who felt he had spent all night trotting after Father Anselm with his heart thumping, came up behind him once more, and once more they stood shoulder to shoulder.

In the long grass, in a little patch of ground immediately beside the corner of the high barn, lay a lamb. Like Brother Dominic and the Bishop of Mitabezi, it had once been white, but was no longer. Its throat had been cut, and a great gash had been made down its stomach, from neck to tail. The ground around it was slushy with blood, like Flanders fields.

There was a long pause. The Bishop shifted from foot

to foot. Eventually he looked at Father Anselm, who was looking at the lamb.

'But if *this* is what Mitabezi had been at,' said the Bishop, 'then who . . . ?'

But he was interrupted by a thunderous knocking at the gate.

CHAPTER VII

CHIEF INSPECTOR PLUNKETT

As THE FIRST RAYS of sunlight were flooding the distant moors with gold, Father Anselm drew back the bolts of the gate, and opened it to the Law. The first representative of that much-invoked abstraction to meet their eyes was a stalwart police sergeant, all shoulders and stomach, his fist upraised to inflict further punishment on the gate, the expression on his face being more or less equivalent to saying, "'Ullo, 'Ullo, what's all this 'ere then?'"

'Come in, come in,' said Father Anselm, gesturing them forward with his hands. 'I'm grateful to you for getting here so quickly. Let me lead the way.'

Enter first, with all the natural dignity of a Victorian beadle, the police sergeant. Enter next someone decidedly higher up the scale, fair, smooth, remote. Enter last, creating his own bustle, something much smaller than either – more wizened, more huddled. Beside the sergeant he looked like a ferret beside a grizzly bear.

'Show me!' the figure barked, for all the world as if he were Julie Andrews.

Father Anselm looked as if he wanted to say something, but the police ferret was already marching in the direction of the main building, looking from behind very much like an undersized adolescent playing at being a Hitler storm-trooper. He hardly seemed, at this moment, a character to argue with. Father Anselm sighed, and followed him.

The Bishop's mind fluttered between two courses. On the one hand, he felt that as one who had witnessed the unepiscopal behaviour of the Bishop of Mitabezi, it was his business to accompany Father Anselm and the two policemen. On the other hand – and how pressingly that other hand always presented itself to the Bishop! – he felt an overwhelming desire to go back to bed. Such conflicts in the Bishop almost invariably resulted in a victory for his overwhelming desires, and such was the case now. He put himself gratefully to bed with the dawn chorus, though not before he had fished from his suitcase a bottle of something and taken a long draught of whatever it was.

Father Anselm did not notice his absence. He led the way to the door of the Great Hall, and let the policemen observe the bloody handle. The door had swung to, and he let them open the door themselves, as best they could, without disturbing the tell-tale stains. Then, unflinching, Father Anselm led the way across the hall, and into the dark corridor leading to the dear departed brother's bedroom. He stood aside at the door, and let the policemen view the body without commentary on his part. In the dim, religious light he merely observed the three of them from behind hooded lids, and his face gave no indication of what opinion he might have come to.

The senior man advanced into the room, and then walked abruptly twice around the bed. The fair man merged with the long shadows in the corner of the room, but his eyes showed he was taking in every detail of the scene, and committing it to memory. The ferret stood a minute or two in intense meditation, and Father Anselm thought he could see his mouth twitching. Finally he spoke again.

'Phone!' he barked. Father Anselm bowed his head – his characteristic gesture – and led the way back to his office.

'Chief Inspector Plunkett here,' the policeman said in his Field-Marshal Montgomery voice as soon as he got through. 'Right! I want photographers. I want fingerprint men. I want doctors. I want the whole caboodle. Right? Got that? At once.'

He banged the phone down.

'You didn't tell them where to,' the police sergeant said.

Chief Inspector Plunkett glared at him, picked up the phone again, and barked : 'We got cut off. Are you getting me? Right. We're at the –' he paused, and seemed somehow to be clenching his teeth – 'the Community of St Botolph's. Right? I'll send Forsyte to the gate. Right.'

During all this, Father Anselm had been getting a better look at Chief Inspector Plunkett. He was not an impressive figure, nor even a prepossessing one. For a start he was small – perhaps not absolutely small, but as policemen go. Perhaps, just as American Presidents are said to grow into their job, he had shrunk out of his. His uniform fitted badly, his complexion was like yesterday's porridge, and he was losing his hair unevenly – in some places it had decided to put up a brave display of growth, in other places it had dispiritedly given up the struggle. His face was hollow, baggy, with eyes that sometimes seemed withdrawn in abstract contemplation, at other times to assume a look of rodent-like cunning.

The call over, Chief Inspector Plunkett despatched Sergeant Forsyte to the gate ('Got that? Right. Be off!') and threw himself down into Father Anselm's chair behind the desk. As an afterthought he motioned Father Anselm himself towards the other chair in the room. After a moment of hesitation, Father Anselm sat down. His manner was becoming frosty, the line of his lips thinner. As he sat he gave Plunkett the sort of look that would have sent the Bishop of Peckham, in his current state of mind, off into a fit of hysterical apologetics. The look had no effect on Chief Inspector Plunkett.

'His name?' he snapped, with something of the parade-ground still in his manner.

'Brother Dominic,' answered Father Anselm, in his deep-frozen voice.

Chief Inspector Plunkett allowed a pause of a couple of seconds, then said in a voice that made no attempt to be pleasant : 'I presume he had a real name?'

Father Anselm furrowed his brow. 'I believe his name in the world was Denis Crowther,' he said finally.

At this phrase 'in the world' Chief Inspector Plunkett licked his tongue round his lips like a lizard. Then he said: 'And his position?'

'He was my personal assistant.'

'I see.'

'And my probable successor.'

'No ordinary brother, then.'

Father Anselm shot him a look. Plunkett was making no attempt to be soothing, or conciliatory: what was odder, there seemed something not far from a sneer in his voice. To let him know that he registered it, Father Anselm paused, before replying: 'We do not make distinctions here.'

'Really?' said Plunkett. 'But nevertheless you had marked him out as your successor?'

'His was one of the names I have mentioned to the Bishop of Leeds. It is the Bishop who has the ultimate responsibility of nominating the head of the Community. He almost invariably takes the advice of the previous incumbent of the position, if it is available. The usual method in the Community is therefore to mention a few names as possibilities, perhaps changing them periodically every three or four years, if for example death has intervened. This method prevents confusion in the event of the sudden death of the head of the Community. If, on the other hand, I decided to surrender office during my lifetime, I would of course discuss the matter in great detail with the Bishop.'

This long speech had not been made directly at Chief Inspector Plunkett. It seemed as if Father Anselm preferred not to look at him. At the end of it, Plunkett leaned forward in his desk, his eyes on the crucifix on the cupboard at the far end of the room, and seemed about to ask a question. But after a long silence, in which the small gold cross seemed to hold his eyes with a magnetic attention, Plunkett shook himself and seemed to try to drag his mind back to the matter in hand.

'Who sleeps in this part of the building?' he asked.

'I myself, and then any guests we have. They sleep upstairs in the guest wing.'

'But you sleep down here, do you?' Plunkett leaned back in his chair. 'Where? Next to him?'

'That is so,' said Father Anselm.

'Hmmm. Why?'

'He was my personal assistant,' said Father Anselm, whose austerity of manner had now reached Crippsian proportions.

'Hmmm,' said Plunkett again.

Walking along the tree-lined path with the assembled technicians, Sergeant Forsyte said to no one in particular: 'There's going to be trouble with this case.'

'What do you expect?' said the fingerprint man. 'Murder's not a parking offence.'

'There's going to be trouble with Plunkett. We're not going to be able to cover up for him this time.'

'Why should there be trouble? I know they keep him off cases with blacks, but there won't be any of them here.'

'Religion,' said Sergeant Forsyte gloomily. 'It's one of the bees in his bonnet. If we're not careful there'll be an almighty stink.'

'What's the matter, Forsyte? Are you embarrassed for the credit of the force?' said the doctor, with a little guffaw, for it was well-known that Sergeant Forsyte, if not exactly bent, was hardly ideally straight.

'I'm afraid of scandal,' said Forsyte. 'And where does that leave us? Subjects of scrutiny, that's what. If he goes down, others may go down with him. We'll have to get Croft to pass the word on higher up.'

'Ah well, Plunkett's Last Case,' said the doctor. 'Let's

hope it's a good 'un.'

By this stage of the interview Father Anselm was standing up. He towered over Chief Inspector Plunkett, glooming, gaunt, and disapproving. If he hoped to gain thus a moral advantage, or to intimidate the policeman, he seemed for once to have failed. Plunkett hardly seemed to notice him, being wrapped in contemplations of his own, from which questions occasionally emerged, but ones which needed some sort of key, if their rhyme or reason was to be discovered. Father Anselm felt he was beginning to have a notion of what that key was.

'If you have nothing more to ask me,' said Father Anselm, after an unusually long period of silence, 'I shall go to my bed.'

Plunkett turned his head in his direction, blinked for a few seconds as if trying to remember who he was, then said, 'Not on your life.' He dragged a packet of cigarettes from his pocket, and lit one with hands that were not quite steady. Father Anselm (who, if the truth were known, would very much have liked a smoke himself) remained immovable, and tried to conceal his strong feelings of distaste.

'That blood on the door-handle,' said Chief Inspector Plunkett, after a couple of draws. 'How did it get there?'

'I have reason to believe,' said Father Anselm, 'that it came off the hands of the Bishop of Mitabezi.'

'Mitter-whatsit?' said Chief Inspector Plunkett.

'Mitabezi,' said Father Anselm, quite naturally. 'It's a province in Central Africa, I believe.'

'Africa.' Plunkett darted his tongue around his lips in a now familiar manner. 'And would this . . . er . . . Bishop of Mitabezi be a . . . coloured gentleman?'

'He is an African, yes,' said Father Anselm.

A dreadful smile came over Chief Inspector Plunkett's face, more terrible than any of his previous expressions, because it revealed his teeth, like two semi-circles of druidical stones which had not been taken under the protection of the Department of the Environment. 'Well,' he said, expanding into geniality and almost rubbing his hands, 'I suppose that's pretty conclusive. If you know the blood is his, the case is as good as closed. Eh? I'll just collect Forsyte and Croft, and then you can take us to him. Right?'

'I fear not,' said Father Anselm slowly.

'Why not? Don't tell me the bird has flown.' Chief Inspector Plunkett turned round as the door opened and Inspector Croft came in, quiet, cat-like as usual. 'The blood belongs to some black bishop,' said Plunkett to Croft. 'And they've let him go.'

At the mention of a black bishop, Father Anselm thought he saw a flicker of apprehension pass over Croft's face. It was the first sign of human emotion he had discerned.

'I did not say we had let him go,' he explained. 'I meant that it's not as simple as that. The blood came from the Bishop of Mitabezi's hands, but it is not, I think, the blood of Brother Dominic.'

'God in heaven, man,' said Chief Inspector Plunkett with pardonable exasperation. 'How many corpses have you got lying around here tonight?'

Father Anselm explained, in a level, passionless tone, the appearance of the Bishop of Mitabezi at the hall door, the blood, the chanting, the putting him to bed – and the finding of the slaughtered lamb immediately before the police knocked at the gate. Plunkett listened avidly, his lizard tongue sometimes flitting out to wet his lips, his pitted brown hands now quite obviously shaking. At the end of the narrative he cast off some of his hard-boiled shell, and let it become clear that he had been impressed.

'So what you're saying is, there was some sort of ritual sacrifice of this lamb, eh?'

Father Anselm nodded.

'It doesn't surprise me,' said Plunkett, with something close to relish. 'If you'd seen the things I've seen, eh, Croft?' Inspector Croft made no response, and looked as if he would infinitely rather not have been consulted.

Plunkett pulled himself away from the contemplation of what he had seen, or thought he'd seen, and tried to focus his mind on the business in hand. 'So what it boils down to is this : last night, for some reason no doubt connected with some disgusting tribal custom, he slaughtered a poor, innocent lamb, and then – what? – then he went on and slaughtered your Mr Denis Crowther? Eh?'

Father Anselm sighed, and it was not for Plunkett's determined secularization of Brother Dominic. 'That is for you to prove, of course,' he said.

'Exactly! Won't take much proving either.'

'But I should have thought that so far we have proof only that the Bishop killed the lamb. And of course, as for that business, the Community will not press charges.'

'So I presume you don't think he also killed your secretary-valet, eh?' asked Chief Inspector Plunkett in a bellicose manner. 'Why, may I ask?'

'The blood around the barn. He made no attempt to hide it – from what we observed, he was in no condition to do so : he was completely in a trance. There would certainly have been some blood leading from Brother Dominic's room, if he had murdered him in the same state. But as you will have observed, there was none.'

Chief Inspector Plunkett muttered something in Croft's direction that sounded suspiciously like 'Father Brown'. Then he said : 'I suppose you also know who it was, if it wasn't the black.'

It went through Father Anselm's mind that the Chief Inspector's manner had passed beyond the limits of allowable police rudeness, and that he ought to complain to his superiors and get him taken off the case – and preferably off any case. Then it struck him that it was hardly up to the suspects to choose their own detective – and anyway . . . He merely answered : 'I have no idea.'

'Anyone could have got into his room?'

'There are no locks on the door – none on any of the doors to the cells. However, the outside door, which you came through, is locked, and the door into the brothers' sleeping wing. For purposes of security. Therefore it does seem certain that whoever it was was someone from this central part of the building.'

'Meaning either you, or one of the guests.'

'Precisely,' said Father Anselm, this time not bothering to proclaim his own innocence. Inspector Croft seemed about to ask a question, but he cast a look at his superior, and seemed to think better of it. Plunkett sat in meditation, his mouth screwed up with effort, or distaste.

'Who are these *guests,* then?' he asked finally.

'They are delegates to a sort of symposium-cum-retreat. The subject is "The Role of the Church in the Modern World".'

'You mean a sort of discussion group?'

'Exactly. We try to keep these groups small, in order not to destroy the atmosphere of St Botolph's. Some of the delegates are English – priests of the Church of England, and the Bishop of Peckham – some are from abroad: America, Africa and Norway.'

'How long have they been here?'

'Two nights.'

'And were any of them acquainted with this . . . Denis Crowther before they came?'

'Not as far as I am aware.'

'Someone seems to have taken an instant dislike then, don't they? Well, I'm going to have to see them all at some time. Have to see how the scientific boys are getting along first. They may have it all tied up. You got any questions, Croft?'

'I presume you've been over how the body came to be found, have you, sir, and what – '

'Yes. Been over all that,' barked Plunkett cavalierly. He waved his hand in Father Anselm's direction. 'You can go.'

Dismissed from his own office, Father Anselm stood for a moment outside the door. That had been a near thing. For Plunkett had not in fact asked him how he came to go to Brother Dominic's room and find the body in the middle of the night. Definitely he would not yet complain to this man's superiors about his conduct of the case.

Turning, he swirled towards the chapel, where he knelt for some time in prayer.

CHAPTER VIII

THE MORNING AFTER

IT WAS PLAIN to Ernest Clayton as soon as he sat down to breakfast that something was wrong. He, unusually, was late, but the Bishop also had only just arrived. He sat hunched over his plate, his eyes paunchy and haunted. He was making hardly a pretence of eating, and was spending his time crumbling his bread on to his plate.

And he was not reacting at all to Randi Paulsen, who was in chirpy, spread-the-word-good-people mood. She was expounding at great length to Stewart Phipps (in a state of proletarian depression, and eating avidly to keep his mind off it) the special problems created by the large sea-going population of Norway.

'Of course we have missions in all the major centres of the world, with resident chaplains, and a truly cosy atmosphere. I myself have helped to select some of the Christian reading-matter we make available to the men who come there, which has been a great joy. But so many of them are rootless young men, without families to go to when they return to Norway, or cut off from them by some sad misunderstanding or other, and the temptations for these young men when they get to the shore ports are really terrible. Sometimes they are drunk for *days*. I suppose with so many large ports in Britain your church must face the same problem?'

Stewart Phipps said 'Urg', or possibly 'Mng' – at any rate he made a noise somewhere between an assent and a protest.

'Naturally the people mainly concerned with the problem are the social welfare people in our church,' pursued Randi regardless, squeezing a smile out to others in the vicinity to bring them in on the monologue. 'We're just beginning a determined campaign to make sure that these men should be offered a real alternative to drink and . . . *worse* . . . when they are on shore. We're recruiting families with a really Christian atmosphere in the home to offer hospitality and even accommodation to these poor boys, and make them feel part of one big Christian family. We're launching the campaign very shortly, and we're using the slogan "Bring a Sailor Home for Christ".'

It was at this point that there should have issued from the Bishop of Peckham's place an ecstatic gurgle, a cockerel chortle, a delirious whinny. No such sound emerged. The Bishop went on crumbling his wholemeal bread and looking at his plate. It was then that Ernest Clayton knew there was something wrong.

He was not to be long in finding out what. A minute or two later Father Anselm stalked across the floor of the Great Hall towards High Table, and placed himself imposingly at the end of the dais. Unlike the Bishop his appearance gave to the casual observer no sign of his night-long ordeal. Such things, his manner seemed to proclaim, were all in a night's work at St Botolph's.

'I'm afraid I have terrible news for you,' he said, without fuss or preliminaries, in a low but impressive voice. 'During the night there has been a murder – of my assistant Brother Dominic, whom you all knew.' He paused and let his eye roam around the faces turned towards him. 'The police are already here and working on the case. For the moment we are in their hands. I suggest that you cancel the discussions arranged for today and make yourselves available to the police if and when you should be called on.'

He let his fine, unfathomable eyes dwell on them and on their reactions of incredulity, horror and distaste for a few seconds more, and then turned to go. But he had not entirely quelled them. He was prevented by Simeon P. Fleishman.

THE MORNING AFTER 81

'Are you telling us there's been a murder?' he asked, his voice rising with incredulity. 'He-arre?'

'That is so,' said Father Anselm.

'But the police can't want to interview *us*,' pursued Fleishman. 'We're strangers here. We hardly knew the . . . young man. For heaven's sake, we're all clergymen.'

'I wouldn't wish to anticipate the Inspector's wishes,' said Father Anselm. 'It is to him that you must put such points. I merely suggest you make yourselves available to him if and when necessary.'

Ignoring further expostulations and questions, he strode down from the dais and towards the brothers breakfasting at the other end of the hall. Here, once again, he addressed them earnestly, but at greater length. He kept his voice so low that nothing could be heard by the delegates at High Table.

Where, in any case, the breakfasters were in a state of considerable shock. Randi Paulsen hazarded the opinion that the news was 'dreadful' and 'quite shocking'. The others were not able to dissent from this view, though Bente Frøystad seemed to bite back a sharp comment. Once Brother Dominic had been sung to his rest on wings of cliché they all got down to discussing the effects on themselves.

'To my mind the sooner we wind up the whole damn symposium and get out of here, the better,' said Simeon Fleishman, whose linguistic patterns seemed to be changing under the pressure of this novel experience. 'Being mixed up in something like this is poison – the mud sticks around you like a bad smell.'

There seemed to be pretty general agreement with this, though no one else was willing to put the matter in such worldly terms.

'Certainly any discussions would inevitably seem a bit beside the point at the moment,' said Ernest Clayton, his eyes straying to the other end of the hall where Father Anselm was still addressing the brothers, who were looking at him intently. 'I suppose that the best we can hope for is that –'

He was interrupted – and so, at the other end of the hall, was Father Anselm, the set of whose body exuded displeasure – by the figure of Chief Inspector Plunkett. His walk as he entered the Great Hall had something of the quality of a goose-step – cocky and aggressive. He sited himself in the open space between High Table and the other eaters, and he said in a voice just that much louder than necessary : 'Right!' His favourite word certainly succeeded in getting him everybody's attention, though Father Anselm gave him the sort of look a German music lover gives someone who says that *Faust* is his favourite opera. In the silence that followed, Plunkett let his rodent's eyes travel slowly and suspiciously round to every corner of the hall. As he intended, everyone who was not quailing before, quailed now. As he brought his attention back to more immediate prospects, his mouth twisted into an unpleasant expression of contempt.

'Right,' he said again. 'I gather you all know what happened last night. Eh? Murder. Right. Now, I'll want to talk to you – ' here he turned to the party at High Table – 'one after another. In alphabetical order. Before that I've got an interesting conversation lined up with – ' here he paused to make quite certain that none of the breakfasters at High Table was black – 'with another of your group. Then I'll send for you. OK?'

They all nodded miserably. Satisfied with having thoroughly intimidated them, Plunkett turned towards the mass of robed and cowled figures at the other end of the hall, and his voice, already too loud and harsh for such an environment, now seemed to have been subjected to a further twist of the volume-control knob. It was almost as if he knew that such a volume, and such a tone, were unheard of within the precincts of the Community, and that he was enjoying himself. There was a mute gesture from one of the older brothers – actually Brother Jonathan

– and there were anguished looks on the faces of some of the others, who resembled nothing so much as deaf men who had suddenly recovered their hearing during a performance of the *1812 Overture*.

'Now! You lot!' said Chief Inspector Plunkett. 'So far as I can see, I may not need to talk to you at all. But you never know what we might uncover. I'll expect you to be available.' Turning towards the door, he paused for a moment, and then said : 'So don't go away!'

With which fatuous command he bustled out of the hall, followed by Sergeant Forsyte. The euphoric expression on the face of the latter could be accounted for by the fact that he was treasuring up every detail of his chief's conduct for retailing to higher authority before many days were out. And he was expecting by then to have such a store – such a store.

The Bishop of Mitabezi was a pitiful sight, and not a pretty one. He had been released from his strait-jacket of bed-clothes (the knots of which had been tied so effectively by Father Anselm that Sergeant Forsyte struggled with them for quite ten minutes), and now he lay on the stripped bed. The first things that met the eye were his hands and robe caked with dried blood. Hardly less remarkable was his expression, which was woebegone and hideously ashamed. He didn't know where to put his face while he was being untied. Unfortunately it was almost impossible, in the tiny room, to put it anywhere where it could not see Chief Inspector Plunkett, who was sitting on a chair drawn up beside the bed, and regarding the discomfited Bishop with an expression on his face so close to a sneer that it was the very last thing to restore the poor man's self-respect.

When he was untied Plunkett allowed him a minute or two to inspect his blood-stained hands and robe, regarding him sardonically from a chair the while. Then he said : 'And now, perhaps, you'd like to tell me what you've been doing? Eh?'

There was a long silence, during which the Bishop of Mitabezi could be heard swallowing convulsively. At last he said: 'I don't . . . exactly . . . remember. But I think I must have . . . killed something.'

'Ye-es,' said Plunkett, with an intonation which said, 'Go on – and the rest.'

'I think it may have been a . . . lamb,' said the Bishop. 'Could that be what . . . this is?' He held up his black-brown hands and looked at them with an expression of guilt that would have been comical to someone with a sense of humour. Chief Inspector Plunkett did not relax the expression of twisted contempt that was now suffusing his face.

'A lamb *was* found,' he said. Then he leant forward, and went on, his voice rising in pitch and volume: 'Found with its throat cut, and a great long slit down its belly. That was you, was it?'

The Bishop sighed, a luxurious moan in the bass clef. 'I'm afraid it must have been. I felt it coming on. Earlier in the day. When we visited the farm and saw all the animals. I . . . felt it. Perhaps I should have said something. But how could I? What would people have said?'

'Blood-lust,' said Chief Inspector Plunkett, his voice cracking with excitement. From the way his tongue sped round his mouth, moistening parched lips, it seemed like a blatant case of the pot and the kettle. The Bishop looked down, ashamed.

'It was the night of the seventh moon. We had a tradition in our tribe . . . All the young men . . . A sort of initiation. Of course I renounced all such things when I became a Christian. All of us did. And yet, somehow . . .'

Plunkett was not willing to leave the i's undotted. 'You get overcome by the thirst for blood,' he said, his voice still dangerously excited.

'I don't know,' said the Bishop. 'I suppose so. The killing was always done by a tribal warrior. In . . . what you would call a trance. I have never been a warrior, but I fear I must have gone into such a trance last night.'

'It's happened before?'

'Yes, once. It didn't get out, of course. And in my own country it would not have been considered . . . so extraordinary. But here . . .'

'And you remember nothing?'

'No, nothing,' said the Bishop, hanging his head.

'Not killing the lamb?'

'No.'

Inspector Plunkett leaned forward. 'Not killing Denis Crowther, known here as Brother Dominic?'

The Bishop started, and looked him straight in the eye for the first time. 'I beg your pardon?'

'This . . . Brother Dominic. Last night he was butchered. Carved up. Have you forgotten that too?'

The Bishop of Mitabezi drew himself up. He had at his command a very considerable dignity of manner, and a great deal of it returned to him now. His fleshy but impressive body stiffened against the wall, and he looked hard and direct at Chief Inspector Plunkett.

'You forget that I am a Christian,' he said.

The Bishop of Peckham, in the period of waiting for Chief Inspector Plunkett to interview him, loafed around the buildings and grounds of St Botolph's, a picture of misery and uncertainty. Several people tried to speak to him, but they got little more than grunts in reply. He went into the chapel and prayed for a while, but while his words flew up his thoughts remained below. To be more specific, he was disturbed by the presence of Simeon Fleishman, apparently also offering up supplications to his non-denominational creator, but in fact letting his eyes dart everywhere around the magnificently austere chapel. So the Bishop gained singularly little peace of mind from the exercise, and resumed his loafing, his eyes also, gaunt from lack of sleep and haunted by the sights of last night, roving everywhere in search of comfort and reassurance.

Finally it was Ernest Clayton who took pity on him. He had an old-fashioned belief in the healing power of nature, and in the notion of 'getting things off your chest'. He took the Bishop by the arm and said : 'Come on – let's go for a walk on the moors.'

The Bishop let himself be taken with only the mildest of protests : 'You don't think the Inspector will want me? He said alphabetical order, didn't he? Do you think I will be F for Forde or P for Peckham?'

'Whichever you are,' said Clayton, 'there'll be time for you to have a walk. I should be first – at least, after Father Anselm, if he hasn't talked to him yet. But I don't imagine there'll be any harm done if we get out of alphabetical order. We'll stay within the grounds, and the walk will do us both good.'

They walked out of the Great Hall, the Bishop flinching at the sight of the door-handle, with its blood and finger-print powder, through the kitchen garden and out on to the moors. Conversation did not flourish at first, and the Bishop did little more than punctuate Clayton's observations with such responses as 'appalling', 'dreadful thing', 'shocking', and so on. But when eventually they got out into the open, and trod the narrow path through the purple heather, Clayton finally said : 'Would you like to tell me all about it?'

The Bishop took a deep breath, as if it was the first of really fresh air for hours, and said : 'Yes, I would. I must tell someone, or – goodness me! – I shall burst!'

And so it all came out. The being woken in the small hours. Father Anselm's overbearing manner, and the nightmare trip to view the bloody remains of Brother Dominic. Then the horror piling on horror, as in a Eurovision Song Contest : the Bishop of Mitabezi's ghastly chant and blood-dripping hands, the call to the police, and the final discovery of the slaughtered lamb. Out here in the open, with the grouse fluttering plumply from clump to clump, the story gained an added air of improbability, of a trumpery piece of gothic horror. If it had not been for the police, and the bloody door-handle, the Bishop might have expected Ernest Clayton to tell him that it was all a nightmare, and that he must have eaten something at dinner that disagreed with him.

But at the end of the recital Clayton merely shook his head: 'Absolutely fantastic,' he said. 'It seems to me quite admirable that you kept your head.'

'I'm not *quite* sure that I did,' said the Bishop mournfully. Then he perked up a little. 'But perhaps I seemed to behave worse than I did only in comparison with Father Anselm. There's a nerve of steel, goodness me, yes! It was as though nothing could surprise him. He took it all without a moment's flinching or hesitation.'

'I see,' said Ernest Clayton.

'But I – couldn't,' said the Bishop of Peckham. But again, he brightened up. 'Still, when all is said and done, I didn't absolutely *mis*behave. I didn't *funk*.'

'I expect there are plenty of us who would have done just that,' said the Reverend Clayton encouragingly. 'One never knows in advance how one is going to behave in a totally unexpected situation. One thing puzzles me a little: I don't see why Father Anselm decided to involve you at all.'

'Well, he felt he had to consult me, you see – since I am the unofficial leader of the symposium.'

'Yes – I can see that Brother Dominic was a member of the symposium, or at any rate, that he was attending the sessions. But first and foremost after all, he was a member of the Community. And as far as I can see this is mainly a Community affair. Some grudge or personal tension that had built up. Quite dreadful, of course, in a religious order – but still, not unnatural, in the circumstances: it is just this sort of set-up where things get out of proportion.'

'I'm afraid it's not as simple as that,' said the Bishop. 'You see, the main block of the buildings is locked off at night from the wing where the rest of the Community sleeps. Brother Dominic and Father Anselm sleep in the main part, but otherwise there's only the guest-rooms upstairs. You can see why I had to be involved – the murderer must be one of our party, either the poor Bishop of Mitabezi, or one of the others. That's why he called me in.'

'I see,' said Ernest Clayton again, in a voice even more studiously non-committal.

'Of course, it could have been Father Anselm,' said the Bishop. 'I think he sleeps more or less next door. But as he said – in that austere way of his . . . rather terrifying, really – as he said, as far as *he* is concerned, it must be one of us.'

'Yes, I take the point,' said Ernest Clayton cautiously. He turned over in his mind the various possible reasons for Father Anselm having drawn the Bishop into the affair. Then he decided to come a little further into the open.

'Did Father Anselm explain how he came to go to Brother Dominic's cell in the middle of the night?' he asked.

The Bishop opened his mouth in a spontaneous gesture of surprise. 'Goodness me, I never thought of that. You mean, how did he come to find the body at all? But it's hardly something I could have asked him straight out, is it?'

'It's something *someone* should ask him,' said Clayton. 'I hope my first impressions of that policeman were wrong.'

'He hardly seems – sympathetic,' said the Bishop.

'He can be as unsympathetic as he likes, so long as he's competent. The trouble is, I don't feel sure – having watched his performance this morning – that he's that. However, I may be entirely wrong.'

'The terrible thing is – thinking it must be one of us,' said the Bishop, nervously wringing his hands, as he did when people came to him with their sexual problems. 'Not because I *like* all the delegates, because, well, frankly . . .' He let his voice fade into an eloquent silence which made his opinion plainer than words could. 'But still, I am in a

way the leader of the symposium, and the thought that
we have come to this little Community and brought
murder into it . . . And *such* a murder too,' he added, his
hands fluttering at the memory of the slashed body on the
bed, and the blood. 'You see, in a way Father Anselm is
quite right : I *am* responsible.'

Ernest Clayton thought it time to reveal to the Bishop
that he had had the wool pulled over his eyes, if that was,
indeed, precisely the nature of the process.

'This business of the locked door to the brothers' dormitory wing,' he said. 'Shouldn't we look into the arguments
there a little more closely? Now, assuming we accept Father
Anselm's word on this, and assuming he did in fact lock
the door last night at the usual time (whenever that may
be), what guarantee does he have that none of the brothers
was hidden in the main building at the time he locked it?'

The Bishop stared at him. 'You mean . . . ?'

'And remained in the main building all night. How does
he know there was no one?'

'I've no idea,' said the Bishop. 'Could he have searched,
perhaps?'

'Odd he didn't mention it, if so. And in any case, the
corridors around Brother Dominic's room are dark at the
best of times. Darker still at night, no doubt. Anyone could
have hidden there at the time he locked up. And a resident
brother would know them like the back of his hand, so the
darkness would be no problem. Come to that, he could
have hidden in the Great Hall, or in the chapel.'

'I don't *think* there was anyone in the Great Hall, not
when we were there,' said the Bishop.

'The chapel would be better,' said Ernest Clayton. 'More
hiding places. In any case, *after* the murder, the murderer
could very easily have gone out. The door to the Great Hall
is locked from the inside.'

'Of course,' said the Bishop.

'And that raises another possibility,' said Ernest Clayton,
pursuing his argument remorselessly, and leaving the usually

agile-minded Bishop of Peckham panting behind him: 'How did the Bishop of Mitabezi get out of the main building?'

'Well, of course, he must have unlocked the door from the inside, as you just suggested the murderer could have done, when he went out to do . . . what he *did* do,' said the Bishop.

'Precisely. But when? At what time did he go out? And how long was the door open?'

'Goodness me,' said the Bishop. 'None of this occurred to me. You're quite a detective!'

Ernest Clayton forbore to say that he was only detective enough to see the obvious fact that the wily Bishop had been the victim of a confidence trick, in which his reason, already upset by the sights he had seen, had been deceived by the speed with which the cards were flashed before his eyes. He merely said: 'The fact is, from the time the Bishop went out (and we don't know when that was) until the time the police came, the door was open, and anyone could come in or go out. It would be worth finding out how easy it is to get out of the brothers' dormitory wing. Of course, the fact remains that the most *likely* murderer may be one of us. Nevertheless, if we ignore the physical circumstances of the murder, and look merely at the general set-up and the psychological probabilities, then the most likely murderer would surely be one of his fellows in the Community.'

'You're quite right,' said the Bishop.

'That being so, the business of how long the main door was unlocked, and whether anyone was hidden in the main building at the time of locking up, becomes important.'

'You think we should go straight along to the police and put these things to them, do you?' said the Bishop hopefully.

Ernest Clayton thought for a moment. 'No, I'm not sure we ought to do that,' he said. 'It would look as if we were trying to get ourselves out of a hole. And as if we were trying to teach them their business. What, frankly, was your impression of the Chief Inspector?'

The Bishop shook his head, and something of his old impishness of manner returned to him. 'A chief scout who has let his position go to his head?' he suggested.

'I suspect that may be putting it mildly,' said the Reverend Clayton. 'Certainly he didn't look as if he would take kindly to being told his business. My own feeling is that, for the moment, we should only bring these points up if the subject occurs naturally in the interview.'

'You could be right,' said the Bishop. 'As modestly as possible, is that the idea?'

'Exactly: casually and tentatively. Of course, if the man is worth his salt he will have seen through the argument — if in fact it has been put to him at all.'

'From what he said to the brothers, I should think it has,' said the Bishop. 'And it sounded as if he's swallowed it.'

'You're right, I'd forgotten that. Well, we'll see. Perhaps he'll be sharper than he looks. At any rate we'd better be getting back so we can find out.'

They were nearly at the farthest wall of the enclosed part of the moor. As they turned to walk back to the distant buildings, Ernest Clayton couldn't help congratulating himself on the change he had wrought in the Bishop's demeanour. There was a spring in the step, a jauntiness in the set of the shoulders, an expression of something near confidence on his face. It was as if he had been given a celestial pick-me-up.

CHAPTER IX

'ALL THIS'

IN SPITE OF the spirit of jaunty optimism which he had managed to foster in the Bishop of Peckham, the Reverend Clayton's own emotional barometer dropped dangerously low in the next few hours. Though he had hitherto had no conscious ambition to play detective, Ernest Clayton had a logical and tidy mind. The information which he had so far gleaned about the occurrences of the night before had been neatly catalogued and cross-referenced in his brain, where also were stored a few cards with possible hints for the future – they had little arrows on them, leading to words with question-marks after them. Such habits of mind had been fostered by, and had been of inestimable use in, the succession of muddles, misunderstandings and petty crimes which had formed the stuff of his parish administration over the last twenty-five years.

To such a mind it is particularly frustrating to be confronted by another which seems unwilling, or possibly unable, to go at a matter straight, keep steadfast to a track, get to the heart of the problem. At first Ernest Clayton tried to believe that there was a hidden design behind the strangely random nature of Chief Inspector Plunkett's questions, or perhaps that he was trying shock tactics. But he found it impossible to cling to that belief as the interview became more and more disorganized. Any idea of subtly planting ideas in Plunkett's mind, superintending their growth, and cheering from the pathway as they burst into flower as if their progress had nothing to do with him had to be abandoned early in the interview. Plunkett was rude, opinionated to the point of obsession, and only at intervals seemed to be interested in conducting a murder investigation.

For what he was really interested in was 'all this', and by 'all this' he did not mean (like the Nancy Mitford character) the outward, visible and comforting signs of wealth and rank. He meant monks, sandals, robes, compline, wholemeal bread, incense – the whole neo-medieval caboodle. And when he spoke of it, a look came into his eyes that Ernest Clayton could only describe as obsessive.

'What do they think they're playing at? Eh?' he would say, his eyes straying to the simple, elegant crucifix on the cupboard in Father Anselm's study. 'Look at that. Doesn't it make you want to spit? But I suppose you approve? Eh? Tell me where you stand.' And he leaned forward and fixed Ernest Clayton with his rat's eyes, his disgusting mouth open as if to catch evidence of Popish leanings.

Luckily at this point they were interrupted by Inspector Croft, who in his silent way padded over to the desk and handed Plunkett a piece of paper.

'The report on the blood samples, sir,' he murmured. Plunkett glanced at it, seemed inclined to crumple it up, but finally pushed it aside with a grunt. He seemed to want to get back to his inquisition of Ernest Clayton, but Croft remained standing there.

'What would you suggest I do now, sir?' he asked quietly.

'Use your initiative. Go and see what you can find at the barn,' said Plunkett, unaware of any contradiction in what he said. Ernest Clayton thought he saw Croft's eyebrows raise themselves a fraction of an inch, but he merely withdrew silently.

Plunkett, reminded of the murder, seemed to be wrenching his mind back to the business in hand. Ernest Clayton – who had been finding it increasingly difficult to hold his temper under the sort of questioning he would hardly allow his bishop to put him through, let alone a layman – helped the process on its way by a question prompted by Plunkett's last command.

'You mentioned the barn,' he said. 'Does that mean you haven't ruled out the Bishop of Mitabezi?'

'Eh?' said Plunkett fiercely. Then he went on : 'Oh, no, the black is out. Well, not out, exactly. Still, there's no evidence. You know what he'd been doing, don't you?' The tongue slicked around the lips. 'Killing a lamb!'

'Yes, I had heard,' said Ernest Clayton. So great was the antagonism the Chief Inspector was arousing in him that for one moment he felt like rushing in with a defence of the practice.

'Have you ever heard anything like it? Eh? But I'd believe anything of them. He'd have killed this Denis Crowther soon as look at him if the fancy had taken him.'

'But you don't think he did.'

Plunkett screwed up his face resentfully. 'There's no more evidence against him than any of you others. All the blood on him was animal. The knife had only been used on the lamb.'

'It hardly seems likely he did it in a trance, then,' said Clayton.

'No, maybe not. Could have done it earlier though, then gone into his little fit and gone rampaging after more blood. Could be you're all lucky to be alive.' His eyes lit up at the thought of all that blood, but then he shook his head regretfully. 'No evidence though. I suppose you didn't see any sign of hostility towards this Denis Crowther from any of the other delegates, as you call yourselves?'

'No,' said Clayton. 'But remember – we'd been here so short a time. We barely knew him.'

'So you say,' said Plunkett.

'If there were any animosities it would be most likely to be from one of the other brothers,' said Clayton.

'Right,' said Plunkett. 'I'd like to have investigated them. I'd have found out a thing or two, never you worry. But they were locked in their wing all night. They're out of it.'

'Unless one of them stayed behind in the main building,' said Ernest Clayton insinuatingly.

'Quite,' said Plunkett, not listening. 'So it's got to be one of you, or this Father Anselm. Have you ever heard the like, though? Locked in at night, like criminals? It's like something out of the Spanish Inquisition.'

The whole conversation was like that.

The Bishop of Peckham was talking to Stewart Phipps when Ernest Clayton emerged from his interview with the Law. They were standing near High Table in the Great Hall, and the sun, streaming through the high stained-glass window, bathed them in strange colours and geometric shadows. They appeared not transfigured, though, but deep in depressed conversation, and Clayton guessed that the Bishop, once his tongue had been loosened, was regaling the whole symposium one by one with the history of his night of horror. He went over towards them.

'Were you grilled?' said the Bishop in a sprightly way. Ernest Clayton had noticed that he seemed always to have a good effect on him, and that he brightened up as soon as he saw him.

'In a way,' said Clayton. 'I had to give an account of my religious position, more especially my attitude towards incense, confession, and I don't know what.'

'But what about the murder?'

'Well, in among all the rest he asked a few questions — more or less at random, or so it seemed to me. He asked whether there was any unpleasantness involving Brother Dominic and any of us. He asked whether there had been anything noteworthy happen the evening before. Oh, yes, and then just before I went he asked what I was doing last night. When I said I was sleeping, he snarled and said, "A likely story." I think by then he must have decided that my religious inclinations were much too high for me to be trusted.'

'He sounds a bully,' said Stewart Phipps. 'He looked like one.'

'I think he is,' said Ernest Clayton.

'Like all the police – a Fascist at heart.'

'It's not a word I like to use,' said Ernest Clayton to Stewart Phipps's surprise – it was a word *he* was using all the time. 'To me the frightening thing about him is partly his incompetence – if it's left up to him this thing will never be cleared up – and partly that I think – well, I don't want to be a scaremonger, but his state of mind seemed to me not so far from madness.'

'Goodness me!' said the Bishop, opening his eyes wide. 'That's putting it strongly, isn't it?'

'You must be as used to the signs as I am,' said Ernest Clayton. 'Not that we see as much of it now as twenty or thirty years ago. There's more football mania these days than religious mania. But to me, that's what it looked like.'

'Religious mania!' said Stewart Phipps, his face creasing into a bitter expression that was really no pleasanter than Plunkett's. 'A murdered monk, a blood-stained bishop, and to cap it all, a policeman with religious mania.'

They all looked at each other. None of them said so, but it seemed to each one of them that the combination of all three elements seemed uniquely designed to capture the imagination of the Sunday paper news hounds.

'Of course, Methodism is very strong in this district,' said the Bishop. 'There are some extraordinary stories from the eighteenth century.'

'Are you implying that Methodists are all religious maniacs?' asked Stewart Phipps, with that same twisted smile. He seemed to have the art of making the Bishop lose his sang-froid: he opened and closed his mouth, positively wriggled with embarrassment, and said: 'No, no. Goodness me, what an idea. I merely meant that he sounded like some extreme fundamentalist. Some little evangelical splinter-group or other. There were many such in the nine-teenth century, and there are lots of them still going strong in the villages around here.'

'You know the area?' asked Ernest Clayton.

'I'm a trustee of the Brontë Society,' said the Bishop.

'Now, the point is, what are we to do?'

'We may have to revise our strategy,' said Clayton. 'This thing can't drag on for ever. The newspapers will make a meal of us. We may be forced to complain higher up.'

'Well, don't rush it,' said Stewart Phipps. 'There may be an article for *Tribune* in this.'

The effect of Inspector Plunkett on the other members of the symposium was to create bewilderment, which in its turn led to alarm and despondency. Bente Frøystad, meeting Ernest Clayton in the kitchen garden, took a great breath of air into her lungs, and then said: 'I need fresh air – after *that*.'

'It's not very nice, is it?'

'Ugh,' she said. 'Only the look. I knew Englishmen had bad teeth, but his are almost obscene.'

'What did he ask you about?'

'All sorts of things – including lots I hadn't expected to be asked about. I had to give him a lecture on the Norwegian Church, with precise details of the services.'

'Do you think he took it in?'

'I don't know. He seemed to perk up when I told him Randi Paulsen belongs to the more evangelical wing.'

'Oh, she does, does she? I thought she seemed a bit – *low*.'

'She's low all right. And, as you will have observed, anti drink, drugs, sex, Catholics, abroad, dancing – you name it, she's against it.'

'I thought that sort of religion was only to be found in the depths of Scotland these days.'

'No, no. We have more than our share. I'm sure Randi will be able to satisfy him on the anti-ritualistic side too. In fact, I can see them having a fine old time getting down to fundamentals.'

'And meanwhile –'

'Exactly. Now what gives? Is the man mad? If he's not, what point is there in all this nonsense he's been asking me about? And if he is, what are you going to do about it?'

She stood there, frank, sturdy and incredulous, her big blue eyes looking directly to him for illumination. Ernest Clayton wished he could say something inspiring, or at least comforting, because he liked the situation perhaps even less than she did.

'All good questions,' he said. 'Wait until the interviews are over, and then we'll have to decide something. I'm sure the Bishop must have contacts who could do something about getting this man Plunkett removed.'

'It's the funniest thing, really,' said Bente Frøystad, her handsome face bursting into a delicious smile, 'when you think of the traditional idea of the English bobby, and then think of the man in there. I wasn't expecting anything like that, I assure you!'

'You didn't have any contacts with the police when you were here as an au pair, then?' asked Ernest Clayton.

'None at all,' said Bente Frøystad, looking straight at him once more with her beautiful blue eyes, which now twinkled, as if to say, 'Has the little man got ambitions to play detective?'

Bente Frøystad, it occurred to Ernest Clayton, took everything in, and gave very little away.

The impressions Philip Lambton had formed of the Inspector seemed no more favourable.

'We didn't seem to be talking on the same wave-length at all,' he said. 'Of course, we couldn't talk about my movements last night for ever, because I didn't *have* any : when I get my head on the pillow I'm out like a light. But he didn't even ask. The only time in the whole interview when we sort of came together was when we got to talking about this ritual slaughter thing.'

'Yes, I had rather gathered he finds that pretty interesting,' said Ernest Clayton.

'Yes, well – in a disgusting sort of way he does,' said Philip Lambton, his naïve face crinkling up into an expression of distaste. 'Now, I find it interesting from lots of points of view, too : I mean, we tend to standardize the ritual side of Christianity, don't we – in fact, we really neglect the theatrical elements almost entirely, sometimes. But here are these new Christian communities in the emerging countries, marrying the old rituals of their – but that's by the way. The point is, the only side this man was interested in was the blood and horror side.'

'Well, that's understandable enough, in view of what he's supposed to be investigating.'

'Yes, but he didn't have to lick his lips so often. And then, there was something so *racial* about his whole attitude.'

'Yes – that came out when he talked to me as well. In fact, the man seems to be a psychological mess.'

'Well, one doesn't want to be uncharitable, but that *was* my impression, I must say. And meanwhile the murder of Brother Dominic seems to go by the board.'

'Precisely,' said Ernest Clayton.

'And though one didn't actually *like* the poor chap . . .'

'No, he wasn't someone one could warm to, was he?'

'Not at all,' said Philip Lambton, without a shred of personal feeling. 'You know, I work a lot among young people, and I get so much pleasure from it because I find them all so open, so forthcoming. I do wish people would see this, and foster it, instead of concentrating on the *minor* things the whole time, don't you?'

'Er, yes,' said Ernest Clayton carefully. 'But certainly Brother Dominic was an exception, wasn't he?'

'Oh, very much so. Of course, he wasn't quite the generation I was thinking of. I imagine he must have been twenty-seven or so.'

'Quite,' said Ernest Clayton, mentally adding 'declined into the vale of years!'

'But he was very much knotted up inside, don't you think, which made him seem much older. He was inhibited, I think – he never *gave*. We don't have young people like that in Liverpool!'

'You had conversation with him, then, did you?'

Philip Lambton did not relax the angelic openness of his expression.

'Only what we had in public – in our get-togethers. He hardly encouraged one to embark on private confidences. I've tried to talk to some of the other younger brothers, when I've met them around the place, but I haven't got very far. They all seem very reserved. None of them seems very curious about the outside world.'

'It is, after all, what they came here to get away from,' said Ernest Clayton.

Randi Paulsen, of course, knew all about Inspector Plunkett before she went for her interview. Nobody felt the need to keep quiet about the oddity of their interviews with him, and, in any case, nothing escaped Randi. No hi-fi enthusiast had an ear better trained to pick up feathery shades of sound that lesser ears might pass over; no naturalist had an eye more used to observing the tiniest movement in the undergrowth. In earlier times Randi would have made a splendid police spy. As it was, her superiors in the Church were delighted with her zeal.

So Randi, in her quick way, had spotted a fellow zealot, and rather expected to enjoy herself. She had, in fact, tentatively mapped out the interview in advance, and when Plunkett said (leaning forward with a show of fellow feeling that at any other time she would have poured her glacial smile over), 'What do you make of all this, then?', she knew exactly how she should reply.

'Well, of course, I am only a guest here,' she said, her thin lips pursing up, 'and it wouldn't be right for me to express an opinion openly, but I must say it's Not What I'm Used To!'

'I'll bet,' said Inspector Plunkett. 'Do you know what I found in this drawer here? A rosary! Think of that. Eh? Doesn't it make you sick?'

The Paulsen lips pursed still closer together: 'I must

say, I'd always thought of the English as a *Protestant* people,' she said.

'There it is, you see,' said Chief Inspector Plunkett, leaning still further forward. 'We're being taken over, that's the point. That's what nobody realizes.'

Though the Inspector was so unpleasantly close, Randi Paulsen's body did not gain further accretions of stiffness, as might have been expected. Indeed, she decidedly relaxed, and prepared to enjoy a lengthy swapping of bigotries.

CHAPTER X

BISHOP TO KNIGHT

THE BISHOP OF Peckham had had heart put into him in the course of the day, and when he finally went in to talk to the Grand Inquisitor, at about half past twelve, he was quite his normal self – avuncular, cheery within limits, but with a definite surface authority. It was thus he behaved on parish visitations. It went down very well with the smaller suburban or country congregations, who otherwise were inclined to be suspicious of so controversial and much-televised a bishop.

It is difficult to say what manner would have brought out the best in Inspector Plunkett. Certain it is that this episcopal manner did not. As the Bishop eased himself down into the comfortable visitor's chair, mopped his brow, and jovially said: 'Dreadful business, this, dreadful,' the submerged sneer on Plunkett's face relaxed not one iota. He was, it seemed, a man whose soul of steel could not be softened by matiness. And when the Bishop said: 'Rely on me for any help I can give,' Plunkett merely replied: 'I suppose you think you're out of it?'

'I beg your pardon?' said the Bishop.

'I suppose you think you're out of the running, eh? – because you're a bishop.'

'Not at all, not at –'

'Because you're not. Not by any means. Bishops don't cut any ice with me. Nor does any of this paraphernalia – robes, sandals, rosaries, crucifixes. No – they don't cut any ice with me.'

The Bishop, uncertain of his wisest approach, made a cat's cradle of his fingertips, and maintained a polite silence.

His attitude, however, seemed only to make Plunkett more aggressive.

'And do you know why it doesn't cut any ice? Do you know why it makes me sick to the stomach? Eh? Because it's popery, that's what it is. Popery. We got rid of popery in this country four centuries ago, and now it comes creeping and crawling back in again, using the Church of so-called England as the back door. If I had my way you'd be chased out of the country – put on the next plane for Rome, where you belong.'

He threw himself back in his chair, and lit a cigarette, almost gasping with eagerness. The Bishop, confronted with the sort of passion he had hardly seen among his co-religionists for years, felt a tinge of fear. Clayton was right. This man was on the edge of insanity. On the other hand, before anything could be done, the interview had to be got through, in as dignified a manner as possible.

'You're quite wrong if you think I expect special treatment,' he said, adding urbanely: 'I've known bishops do some very extraordinary things. You're quite right to suspect me.'

'I suspect everyone in your group.'

'Quite, quite – it's your duty to. No doubt Father Anselm will have told you that I was asleep in my bedroom when he came to inform me of the murder?'

'Oh, he told me. Whether you *were* asleep or not, we don't know, do we? Whether he was telling the truth or not, we don't know, do we? For all I know, you may be in this together. In other words, there may be criminal collusion.'

'Yes, yes,' said the Bishop, sighing. 'I see it must be very difficult to know who to believe.'

'Your real name,' said Inspector Plunkett, leaning forward with a hideous, thirsty expression on his face, as if he were accusing the Bishop of going under an alias, 'is Henry Caradyce Forde, isn't it?'

'Er – yes.'

'You write – *books,* don't you?' The word was ejaculated as if it were a strand of tough steak stuck between his teeth. 'I've read about them, haven't I? Modern books, I believe, isn't that right?' He paused dramatically. 'Heretical books, I'd call them – blasphemous books. Sacrilegious. It's men like you that destroy people's faith!'

For the first time in his life the Bishop regretted the widespread publicity which had been given to his radical reinterpretations of the basic truths of Christianity.

On her way down to lunch Bente Frøystad met up with Randi Paulsen in the corridor outside their bedrooms.

'How did it go?' she asked. 'Was he as crazy with you as with the rest of us?'

Randi was feeling so pleased with herself at the way the interview had gone that she had not prepared herself for such a question.

'He certainly seemed very interested in spiritual matters,' she said primly, and pulling open the door she went into her room.

Lunch was not a happy meal. It was not the food that was the cause : it was excellent plain fare as usual, showing that murder had not disturbed the routine of the kitchen. All ate hungrily, showing that murder did not upset the digestive processes either. Ernest Clayton observed that down in the body of the Great Hall the brothers were doing likewise, and, against the usages of the Community, talking among themselves – eagerly, almost excitedly, like birds about to migrate.

It was the presence of the head of the order which cast a blight over High Table. To begin with it had seemed as if his purpose in coming among them (which he had avoided as much as possible over the last two days) was to reassure them, and restore something of the holy calm of St Botolph's to the atmosphere. So that, though the presence of the ladies still seemed to affect him disagreeably, and though he cast a particularly polar glance in the direction of Bente Frøystad (glowing with vitality and charm, and not bothering with too much simulated grief for the dear departed brother), still, he attempted at the beginning to establish a restful, mournful atmosphere over the table.

But the talk turned to murder, as it could hardly fail to do, and Father Anselm – lacking the human touch that would have told him that this was something he had not had an earthly chance of stopping – retreated into significant silence.

'One thing I would like to know,' said Ernest Clayton, sitting two places away from Father Anselm, and making unavailing attempts to draw him into the conversation, 'is when the Bishop of Mitabezi went out to – do what he did.'

'Why is that?' asked Bente Frøystad.

'Because,' said Clayton meaningfully, 'if it was, say, midnight, that would mean that the main door was unlocked from then until about two-thirty, when the Bishop was seen coming back into the main building by Father Anselm here, and the Bishop.'

If Father Anselm was dismayed to hear his theory concerning the limits on who could be suspected coming under question, he gave no sign, merely gazing at his plate with an expression of distaste on his face, as if he was wondering whether it was the lamb slaughtered by Mitabezi that he was now eating.

'So you mean – ' said Stewart Phipps, his ferrety eyes aglow.

'That is the time anyone could have come in and killed Brother Dominic. I mean, for example, anyone from outside the Community – for the walls are mere child's play – or any of the brothers, if it is possible to get out of their wing at night.'

He looked again towards Father Anselm, who looked straight ahead of him to the empty seat at the other end of the table, usually occupied by the Bishop of Peckham, and gave no sign of having heard. He was clearly too wily a fox to be drawn by such manoeuvres.

'So you mean,' said Randi Paulsen, leaning forwards, and genuinely interested, 'that the murderer might be – just to take an example – a thief from outside?'

'Yes, indeed. The plate in the chapel certainly looks worth anyone's attention. Then again, it could be someone connected with Brother Dominic's past life.'

Ernest Clayton noticed that Simeon Fleishman seemed about to say something, and then stopped. So he went on : 'All this is dependent on times, of course.' He determined that he would have to take the battle into Father Anselm's country. 'What time was it, Father, that you went into Brother Dominic's room?'

There was a long pause. It was apparent to everyone present that Father Anselm resented even so simple and factual a question as *lèse-sainteté*, an impertinent questioning of one who should be beyond trivialities of that kind. There were storm-clouds over the snow. Finally, however, he turned his fathomless eyes in Ernest Clayton's direction and said : 'About ten minutes to two.'

The assembled delegates waited with baited breath to see if the Reverend Clayton dared to ask the next question. The inevitability of that question had been perceived even by Simeon P. Fleishman. Ernest Clayton speared a boiled potato, and said :

'Why did you go to his room at that time of night?'

The silence at High Table was like Frogmore mausoleum waiting for a visit from Prince Albert's relict. From the body of the hall came the whispered chatter of the brothers, like the voices of the distant world outside.

'That is a matter,' said Father Anselm, with simulated calm, 'that I am quite willing to discuss with the proper authorities, should they consider it of importance. You would hardly expect me to discuss it at this time with you.'

Once into deep water, Ernest Clayton decided he had to swim onward and outward. 'It is because the proper authorities seem disinclined to ask the obvious questions that I feel they have to be asked by someone,' he said.

'Then you will pardon me if I doubt whether you are the person,' said Father Anselm, pushing back his chair. 'I have no doubt you are asking these questions as part of some sort of childish game, and I decline to have anything to do with it.' He stood up, towering over them, looking coldly wrathful. 'I have business of more importance to attend to.'

And he stalked the length of the Great Hall, his robe billowing against his lanky body as if in an angry wind. As he went past the lower table, voices were stifled and eyes were lowered, and even after he disappeared into the gloom of the cloisters the brothers seemed to have lost the urge to break their silence.

Not so High Table, which suddenly found they had a great deal to say to each other.

'You realize it's people like you who rob ordinary men and women of their faith, don't you?' said Plunkett, stabbing the cosy, episcopal form of the Bishop of Peckham with his hat-pin eyes. 'Do you realize when I was a boy this was a Christian country? Eh? What is it now? A paradise for pimps and druggies, that's what it is. A haven for rotten Hindus and Moslems, buying our churches for their filthy rituals, shovelling their poisonous foods into our bellies, living off our welfare state. What do you feel like when you walk through the streets of London? Eh? I'd never seen a darkie till I was twenty. Now they're teeming everywhere, I can hardly bear to walk down the street it's so bad. We're being overrun by lesser breeds without the law !'

Thus far the Bishop had been holding his own pretty well. He was used to dealing with fundamentalists, and he had been firm, dignified and (in so far as it was possible to be in such a ludicrous situation) reasonable. As Plunkett swerved crazily off on to new pastures, and he found himself being held personally responsible for the entire process of coloured immigration, a realization came to him that any pretence at rational conversation with a man in his state of mind was out of the question. A great wave of weariness swept over him. At any moment now, he foresaw, the River Tiber would be flowing with much blood.

'Well, our streets would be a lot more dirty if we hadn't the coloured immigrants to sweep them,' he said feebly.

'Huh,' spat out Plunkett, not likely to be mollified by such scraps of liberal leavings. 'They're the litter I'd like to see removed.'

'And I don't know how our hospitals would manage,' said the Bishop, feeling he ought to add: 'Count your blessings.'

'And what do you think those damned blackies are doing in the hospitals. Eh?' yelled Plunkett, his voice rising as he became uncontrollably gripped by all his various hysterias. 'Injecting us with poisons known only to them. They're filling us with drugs to debilitate us. Weaken our resolve to rule! Make us lose our grip! You can see it happening, bit by bit, every day.'

'Inspector Plunkett,' said the Bishop, with some dignity, 'I kept my patience during your investigation of my religious opinions, totally irrelevant though I found it to the matter in hand. I see no reason whatsoever why I should waste my time listening to your peculiarly nasty racial prejudices, or being put into the dock about something which I have not an atom of control over and which has no conceivable relevance to the investigation you are supposed to be making.'

Plunkett's face took on an expression of infinite cunning. 'Him upstairs,' he said, 'he's a darkie. Right?'

'He is coloured,' admitted the Bishop. 'But he is not an immigrant.'

'He's a bishop of your church,' said Plunkett triumphantly.

'No doubt, but I do not see the relevance of that to the present case.'

'You're the enemy within, you see, and he's the enemy without. You're one of the ones sapping away our fibre. You're spreading doubt and irreligion. And he's one of the ones just waiting to take over.' He bared his fangs in a horrible snarl. 'Do you know what I foresee for this country in a few years' time?'

The Bishop took a deep breath.

'The River Tiber flowing with much blood,' said he and Plunkett in unison. It was all too much. The Bishop rose, inclined his head, and made for the door.

The Bishop of Peckham was momentarily exhilarated by his decisive action in walking out of Father Anselm's office, which Plunkett's presence had somehow transformed in his mind into something resembling Alberich's cave. But the feeling did not last. The decisive action had to be followed up by further decisive action – the removal of Plunkett. And, as so often at crisis moments of this kind, the Bishop's resolve turned to jelly. He was really the sort of bishop Elizabeth I liked to deal with.

His instinct was, as had become a habit recently, to consult with Ernest Clayton. He pottered around the grounds and buildings of the Community in search of him, and finally found him in the room which they had used for their few symposium sessions. He was talking to Simeon P. Fleishman, but at the Bishop's approach the American evaporated, in so far as it was possible for so substantial a figure to do so.

'What do you make of our Simeon?' asked the Bishop, so as not to bring out his problems too immediately and appear too dependent.

'A clerical crook?' hazarded Clayton, who knew perfectly well what the Bishop really wanted to talk about. 'To be perfectly honest, I can't make him out. Outside of matters of finance he seems irredeemably stupid. Even with our present shortage of clergymen he'd never get to theological college here. One wonders what on earth his sermons would be like. Probably something like Denis Healey's, I suppose. But what about you? How did it go?'

'Dreadful, dreadful,' said the Bishop. 'A long inquisition concerning my various heresies, done in a very unpleasant manner – almost as if he were a reporter for one of the sensational Sundays. Then he veered round on to coloured immigration, I forget how, and somehow I seemed to be responsible for that too. I'm the "enemy within", whatever he may mean by that.'

'And about the case itself?'

'Nothing. Less than nothing. He didn't seem in the least interested. I'm afraid I'm forced to agree with you. The man is completely off his head.'

'Then he must be removed,' said the Reverend Clayton briskly.

'You think so?' said the Bishop nervously.

'How else will the thing ever be cleared up, and us let out of this place? If we don't get a competent man on the job, it will hang around us like a dirty smell, and people will be gossiping about it behind our backs for years to come.'

The Bishop seemed to hear his hopes of an Archbishopric evaporate into the blue with a flap of angel's wings. 'You're right,' he said. 'What do you suggest?'

'Well, we could start by finding out who the Chief Constable is,' said Ernest Clayton. 'Surely in your position you usually find you can go to the top?'

'True,' murmured the Bishop complacently, and followed Clayton out of the meeting-room, through the dim cloisters, and out into the sunlit expanse of the Great Hall.

'I thought so,' said Ernest Clayton, looking towards the main door, where Sergeant Forsyte was posted, looking hefty and useless and bored. 'See what you can get out of him.'

The Bishop was quite unsure of the manner he should adopt to Sergeant Forsyte, though he needn't have worried, for the good sergeant had more than an inkling of what was on his mind, and a limitless desire to help. 'I'm awfully sorry to trouble you, Sergeant,' said the Bishop, dancing from foot to foot in his embarrassment, 'but I wonder if you could – in short – if you could tell me the name of the Chief Constable of the Riding?'

'Certainly, sir,' said the good sergeant, who didn't know how to address a bishop, but oozed servility instead. 'It's Sir Henry Abbotsford, of Kirkby-le-Dale.'

The Bishop skipped gleefully back to Ernest Clayton. 'It's Harry Abbotsford,' he said. 'I met him at one of the Brontë Society do's – the trip to Scarborough on the Anne Brontë one hundred and fiftieth Anniversary, I think. What a stroke of luck!'

'Then you must get on to him,' said Ernest Clayton.

The Bishop, fired with conspiratorial zeal, jumped to find Sergeant Forsyte suddenly at his elbow.

'The phone number is Kirkby-le-Dale three five six nothing,' said the Sergeant levelly, looking straight into the Bishop's eyes.

'Oh, thank you, thank you,' said the Bishop to his retreating figure. 'Much obliged.'

'Right,' said Ernest Clayton. And then they both stopped in their tracks.

'Where do I phone from?' said the Bishop helplessly. 'The only phone I've seen is in Father Anselm's room.'

'Oh, dear,' said Ernest Clayton, 'I'm sure that's the only one. How stupid of us not to have thought of that. I suppose I could drive you into Hickley.'

'I don't like the idea of that,' said the Bishop. 'They might not let us out – and it would look as if we were running away.'

They both thought for a moment.

'Peckham,' said Clayton thoughtfully. 'I wonder if you were the last. There's no one after you alphabetically. It could be he's left his office – though heaven knows what he might be planning to do next.'

They skulked along the cloisters and ducked into the semi-darkness, watched by the benevolent eye of Sergeant Forsyte. As luck would have it, they were no sooner in the murk of the corridors than they heard the sound of a door being opened. Standing quite still in the long shadow (the Bishop thought that perhaps last night someone had done exactly the same thing, in exactly the same spot, and the thought nearly set his teeth chattering) they saw Chief Inspector Plunkett emerging from Father Anselm's office, his suspicious little eyes darting everywhere. After a moment of indecision, he started off down the little passageway leading to the chapel.

'Now,' whispered Ernest Clayton. 'Kirkby-le-Dale three five six nothing. I'll keep watch at the corner, and I'll cough twice if he comes out of the chapel.'

The Bishop darted into Father Anselm's office, and a moment later Ernest Clayton heard him riffling through the telephone directory for the dialling code.

It was early afternoon, and the Chief Constable had just risen from his after-lunch nap. Such a situation did not normally find him in his best humour, but he dearly loved a Lord, and a bishop was the next best thing. So he my-Lorded him with great geniality, and listened to his story.

'Of course I realize,' said the Bishop in a low, earnest voice, terrified lest Alberich should return to his cave and clobber him with a Nibelung's hammer, 'that a complaint at this stage may seem very premature. But when the man arrived his manner seemed strange, and in the course of the day it has become stranger and stranger. I must say that many of us feel that he is quite literally mad.'

'In what way mad?' asked the Chief Constable, perhaps wondering whether Plunkett was wandering round in white satin, distributing flowers.

'He's spent his entire time asking us about our religious views, and shouting and snarling at us if he doesn't approve

of them. He's made no investigation whatsoever of the
case, as far as I can see. And he's absolutely obsessed about
colour.'

'Colour?' said the Chief Constable, seeming to take more
notice.

'Coloured people. He practically foams at the mouth
when they're mentioned. For some reason he seems to think
I'm personally responsible for letting them into the country,
though beyond the odd remark on *Any Questions?* I don't
recall that I ever – '

'Oh, dear, that's bad,' said the Chief Constable. 'We're
having to be very careful about anything of that kind.
We've had very strict directions from the HO.'

'And of course the Bishop of Mitabezi is here.'

'Oh, good lord, a coloured bishop,' said Sir Henry in
disgust. 'Well, look, I'll get on to this, and if – '

But Sir Henry was interrupted by a noise which even
he, in Kirkby-le-Dale, couldn't fail to register. The Bishop,
so much closer, practically jumped out of his gaiters. It
was a thunderous clang of metal, and it reverberated around
the narrow corridors, and was speedily followed by further,
lesser clangs, all of which left their little shivers of noise
behind them, as if they were part of an acoustics experiment.

'One moment, Sir Henry,' said the Bishop in his normal
voice, and scooted for the door. His intention was to make
for the open, but at the end of the corridor he saw Ernest
Clayton, who beckoned.

'Come on,' he said, and the two went hurrying down
the long dark passage which led to the chapel, Clayton
keeping a comfortable lead. The door was open, and they
stood in the doorway, incredulously watching the figure
inside.

Chief Inspector Plunkett was standing to one side of the
chapel, his hands on his hips, apparently contemplating
his handiwork with satisfaction. He was at the entrance to
a tiny side-chapel, hardly more than a box, with a William

Morrisy stained-glass window. The plate from the altar of this chapel had been hurled to the floor, and the altar cloth dragged after it. A heavy candlestick was still rolling in a sea-sick manner down the side-aisle, and as they watched he reached for a statue of St Botolph, in a small niche.

'Idolatry!' barked the Inspector, to the heavy oak rafters. 'Confounded, damnable idolatry!' And he hurled the statue to the ground.

Then, doing a sharp, right-angled turn, he strode in his military way towards the high altar.

'We must stop him,' whispered Ernest Clayton urgently to the Bishop. But they made no move, whether from understandable doubts of their own capacity to hold the madman, or from a desire to see him struck by celestial lightning for his sacrilege perhaps neither of them quite knew. Reaching the altar, and uttering meaningless little grunts of hatred and contempt, Plunkett seized the massive silver pieces one by one and, casting them down with a certain sense of theatre, sent them crashing and hopping down the altar steps and across the chapel floor. He seized the Sanctus lamp, but was prevented by its chains from hurling it to the floor. Instead a superb brass crucifix fell victim to his Cromwellian zeal. The pieces rang out richly and impressively, and the Inspector sent them on their way with more incomprehensible cries, this time of triumph, presumably over popery.

Finally, hearing sounds from the other end of the corridor which they thought might be Father Anselm, the Bishop and Ernest Clayton decided they could remain quiescent no longer. They advanced purposefully across the chapel just as Plunkett seized the last of the pieces on the altar, a heavy candlestick, and began sending both it and the altar cloth skidding across the chapel floor.

But, progressing up the wide central aisle, the Bishop and Clayton found themselves confronting not just the heavy candlestick, which rolled towards them like distant thunder, but also a lesser object, which skimmed out of the altar cloth and across the floor at them. It scraped the candlestick with a metallic shriek, and finally landed up not far from the door, in which now stood framed the figure of the head of the Community of St Botolph's. The three clerics stood looking at the object.

It was a long, sturdy, deadly-looking knife, and its blade was brown with blood.

It looked as if Inspector Plunkett had found a clue at last.

CHAPTER XI

NEW BROOM

THE DOWNFALL OF Plunkett was done cleanly and speedily – it resembled the whirlwind denouement of farce rather than the long-drawn-out catastrophe of tragedy. At a glance from Ernest Clayton the Bishop had scooted out of the chapel, leaving Clayton to guard the knife from the attentions of both Father Anselm and Inspector Plunkett. Regaining the phone he gave a hurried, urgent account of Plunkett's desecration of the chapel, and Sir Henry Abbotsford emitted a howl of anguish. Within twenty minutes Chief Inspector Plunkett was walking towards the gates of the Community, flanked on either side by a policeman of inferior rank: to all appearances he was simply going about his ordinary business, but it was noticeable how close his two supporters kept to him. Within half an hour his former deputy was in charge of the investigations, and had taken over Father Anselm's study.

The whole operation went very smoothly, and would have impressed the delegates very favourably with the efficiency of the British police force, if they could have forgotten that it was they who had employed and sent Plunkett in the first place.

Inspector Croft was a very different type from his former superior. He was not hysterical, he was not obsessed, he was not incompetent. What he *was*, positively, was more difficult to pin down. He was rather larger than Plunkett, and certainly better looking, but further than that one would be cautious of going. There was something indefinite about his features – they merged into each other, they made no gestures, they were far from easy to describe. Even his eyes were bluey, greyish, almost light brown, and his hair was not quite blond and not quite brown. His manner was a perfect match for his appearance. He asked questions deliberately, listened carefully to the replies, and watched the subject of his interrogation from under rather heavy eyelids.

The conclusion was irresistible: a real investigation was going on. The reactions of the principal suspects were interesting to observe. All of them, naturally, had to express relief that something intelligent and intelligible was being done at last, after the Keystone Cops antics of Chief Inspector Plunkett. But there were, Ernest Clayton felt, degrees of relief. And degrees of apprehension as well. Interesting, too, were the consequences for the cohesion of the group. In their contempt for and dislike of Plunkett they had all been more or less united (though Randi Paulsen had stood somewhat outside the group on this); but now that they were under a real investigation, this unity seemed to crumble, and the tensions and incipient animosities which had been a feature of the first two days of the symposium seemed bubbling once more under the surface, and about to erupt.

Inspector Croft began, as was logical, with the murder, and had from the Bishop of Peckham and Father Anselm an account of the circumstances, and of the nature of the symposium which had brought the diverse people to sleep in the guest-rooms of the Community. The Bishop, in his interview, was direct, detailed, and (so far as it went) frank. If he concealed some of his emotions on the fateful night, that was only human. He was, thought Croft, a good witness on facts, and an intelligent if superficial judge of character. Father Anselm was excellent on the bare facts, but he was not sure he would trust him on character. He was, throughout the interview, dry and formal, not given to expansive detail or explanation. And when Inspector Croft, who was no fool, asked the inevitable question, he got a direct reply, cool and as short as the subject allowed:

'You went to his room at ten to two,' said Croft matter-of-factly, and looking at him from under his hooded lids. 'What was the reason for that?'

Father Anselm gazed directly at him, with his unrevealing eyes.

'We have a tradition at St Botolph's that we are always available to any of our brothers in spiritual distress,' he said. 'Since the coming of the women within our walls, I have been in a state of considerable doubt and perturbation. I went to Brother Dominic so that we might discuss the matter, and eventually pray for guidance together.'

'I see,' said Inspector Croft, and went on to the circumstances of the finding of the body.

In the flurry caused by the change-over in investigator, Ernest Clayton slipped up to the guest wing to have a few words with the Bishop of Mitabezi. Mitabezi was no longer in bed : he had resumed his normal dress (canonicals), and when Clayton knocked he was prowling round the limited confines of his room. He did not know what Clayton had been quick to observe – that the policeman who had been stationed outside his door during the brief reign of Plunkett was now occupied in conveying that deposed monarch into exile, or, to be more precise, to the safe keeping of a nursing home well known to the police force. The Bishop did not quite know how to receive his visitor. He had, in fact, hoped that when the investigations were completed he would be allowed to have himself conveyed from the Community without the need to meet any of his fellow delegates again. Ernest Clayton, too, was somewhat at a loss, so the interview was a prickly one.

'I need hardly say how frightfully sorry we all are about this,' he said, sitting down on the bed in obedience to a reluctant gesture from the Bishop. 'I thought you'd like to know that the maniac who's been running the case has been taken off it – he went completely off his head. No doubt that will be some relief to you.'

The Bishop of Mitabezi looked at him doubtfully. 'I

suppose that means I shall be interrogated again?"

'Perhaps,' said Clayton. 'Very unpleasant for you, no doubt. But no doubt you are as anxious as the rest of us, or more so, that the truth should be established – and at least there is some hope of that now. In any case, so far as I can see you are the one of us least under suspicion.'

There was a pained silence. 'Perhaps,' said the Bishop of Mitabezi, 'but I should greatly prefer not to talk about it again.'

Ernest Clayton (who was fond of animals) nearly said that he would doubtless also prefer not to have done what he had done, but glancing up at the Bishop he thought better of it. There was something about that fleshy bulk that spelt power, and a refusal to brook opposition. A man not lightly to be disagreed with, certainly not lightly to be crossed. In his own environment a man whom high position was not likely to make humble, but increasingly arrogant. Nevertheless, he was not now in his own environment, and he was at something of a disadvantage, and Ernest Clayton decided he would nevertheless ask his question. He did it with a degree of awkwardness, and without looking at his man.

'One thing I'd like to know,' he said. 'It's rather important, all things considered, when you went out to – when you went out. The point is, you see, the door was left unlocked, and anyone could have got into the main building. This would widen the field of suspicion considerably from the members of the symposium – it could even mean an outsider might be involved. I suppose you wouldn't remember – '

'No,' said the Bishop of Mitabezi.

'You wouldn't be able to guess, then? From – from the usual practice of your – people?'

There was silence.

'I think it probable,' said the Bishop, slowly and with some dignity, 'that I may have gone out some time shortly before midnight. But I don't know exactly.'

'I see,' said Ernest Clayton.

'I would be obliged if you would spare me further questions on the subject,' said the Bishop, bowing, clearly in farewell, to Clayton, who rather against his will rose to go. The interview was at an end. Clayton decided that the person the Bishop of Mitabezi most reminded him of was not his fellow bishop, of Peckham, but Father Anselm. They both had the power, in the most adverse circumstances, of making one feel very worm-like indeed. Clayton wondered if this was how Pontius Pilate was made to feel.

Dinner was a meal less fraught with heavy silences than lunch had been. Father Anselm was absent, and High Table speculated rather daringly on the substance of his interview with the new investigator. The Bishop reported on his session with the new man, and judiciously summed up his impressions of him. Clayton noticed that, now the crisis was over, the Bishop was beginning once again to assume a natural air of dignity and authority. Soon, he guessed, he would begin avoiding those who, like himself, had seen him at his worst moments and had the chance to spy out his weaknesses. His report on his interview was delivered not as to fellow-suspects, but as to the lesser clergy of the diocese. He ate well.

So did Simeon P. Fleishman. But then he always did : he ate copiously, with the air of a man who wished he'd thought to bring along a supply of cream biscuits to the Community; he eyed other people's plates and did not scruple to ask for their leavings. He was also talking more expansively today, and was much taken up in his mind with the abrupt departure of Chief Inspector Plunkett.

'Naturally I haven't liked to say anything in any way derogatory,' he said, 'being a visitor to these shores, but he wasn't how we in the States conceptualize a typical British policeman.'

He shovelled into his mouth a whole roast potato and masticated it massively.

'Thank goodness for that,' said Philip Lambton. 'We have some shreds of reputation left, then.'

'Some case,' said Fleishman reflectively, through his potato, 'when the cop goes off his head and starts heaving altar plate around! I'd sure like to have seen that!'

It seemed an odd sentiment, even from a non-denominational clergyman. Philip Lambton felt obliged to say, 'Not my idea of an entertaining show,' and Bente Frøystad agreed: 'Hardly. Quite apart from anything else, they might have been damaged. And they must be priceless!'

Simeon Fleishman forked a thick slice of beef into his mouth, and slowly shook his head.

'Oh, no,' he said, without the slightest sign of embarrassment. 'They weren't of any great value. I gave them the once-over. They were all silver plate, and reproductions of a relatively inexpensive variety. The insurance company won't go broke over that little lot.'

'Popped the silver, eh?' said the Bishop, delighted. Then he realized that this was hardly a dignified reaction. and he twisted his mouth back into a serious shape. 'Of course this is a fairly recent foundation,' he said. 'Very likely they have no great stock of plate.'

The table considered this.

'I have every sympathy with the parishes who are selling their plate and using it for pastoral purposes,' said Stewart Phipps, who, given half a chance, would have sold off any valuables his parish might possess and sent the proceeds to striking Cowley car-workers. 'The idea of a rich church is a hideous contradiction in terms.'

'Very likely that is what has happened here,' said the Bishop authoritatively. He caught the eye of Ernest Clayton, and both of them were thinking the same thing: 'Very likely, my foot!'

And the Bishop was also wondering: 'Wouldn't it be better if the police were told nothing of this?'

Detective-Inspector Croft had been on several murder cases,

and in his experience they divided themselves into three kinds : murders that sprang from an atmosphere of violence in which the victim lived or had strayed – the Belfast or Glasgow type of murder; murder for money; and murder where the victim was asking to be murdered. Since the Community of St Botolph's presumably bore no resemblance whatever to the Gorbals or the Crumlin Road, and since money played little or no part in the lives of the brothers, it was to be presumed that this murder was of the third type. In some way or other – possibly quite unconsciously – Brother Dominic was asking to be murdered. Croft therefore considered it a vital preliminary to any more detailed investigation that he should get some idea of the character of the dead man.

It was not altogether easy. We get our impressions of other people's characters from their behaviour to their wives and families, to their superiors and inferiors at work, to people they meet on trains and in pubs. In the Community of St Botolph's much of this everyday side of human nature had been wiped from the slate. Much of the day was spent in prayer, contemplation and silent work, apparently, and though in these activities the brothers may have laid themselves bare to their Lord, they did not make things easy for a mere mortal police inspector. Croft had got very little from Father Anselm beyond that Brother Dominic was dedicated to his vocation – as presumably all the brothers were – and a highly efficient administrative assistant. The Bishop had said almost nothing, though Croft's sensitive nose had caught a slight whiff of *de mortuis* . . . Now, once again, he was getting very little of any use from Brother Hamish.

Brother Hamish sat in the chair, his hands clasped together, his eyes sometimes in his lap, sometimes at the far wall, never for more than two seconds together looking straight at Croft. He found it difficult to sit still, and in his posture there seemed perpetually to lurk an incipient wriggle. Was it this that reminded Croft of Uriah Heep?

He found it difficult to think of Brother Hamish as a man with a vocation. On the other hand, his daughter went to the local Catholic school, and he had met among the teachers some fearsome nuns whom it was extremely difficult imagining having any vocation other than for the prison service (force feeding branch). Not that Brother Hamish was in any way formidable, as they were. In fact, he wondered if Brother Hamish's vocation to retire from the world arose from an inability to live successfully in it.

'Of course he was enormously dedicated,' said Brother Hamish, looking momentarily at Croft, then down to the carpet. 'You might call him an ascetic. He had no doubts about his vocation, and he was totally satisfied with his life here.'

'Does that mark him off from the other brothers?' asked Croft, curious.

'We're only human,' said Brother Hamish. 'It's only natural to have doubts now and then. Or regrets.'

But not, apparently, Brother Dominic.

'Was he popular with the other brothers?' asked Croft. Brother Hamish's excessively mobile eyes seemed to cloud over.

'Forgive me – I find it difficult to think in those terms,' he said after a pause. 'That is rather a worldly way of looking at things: he wouldn't have thought in those terms himself, and therefore I too would rather not.'

Croft decided it was intended he feel rebuked. He amended his question. 'Were his relations with the rest of you perfectly friendly?' he asked.

'Certainly. Of course.'

'He spoke freely with you?'

'Yes, indeed. Though you must remember that we speak very little here,' said Brother Hamish.

'Naturally, I quite understand that. What do you know about his past life, before he entered the Community?'

Croft caught Brother Hamish's eyes in the middle of their travels, but got nothing from them, except an indefinable suggestion of shiftiness. He felt Brother Hamish had been expecting the question.

'Nothing whatsoever. We do not talk of such things unless any brother particularly wishes to do so. Some few do – some to excess now and then – but most of us prefer not to.'

'Why?'

'We have given up all that,' said Brother Hamish, his eyes diving to the floor again. 'Our minds are on other things.'

'Would you say,' said Croft experimentally, 'that most people came here as a result of some experience in the world – some disillusioning or tragic experience, perhaps?'

'Oh, no,' said Brother Hamish, wringing his hands, and now definitely wriggling. 'No, I wouldn't say that. I believe that most of us have always been interested in religion, and that we have found our vocation gradually – sometimes quite young, sometimes after living in the world for a time.'

'That's how most people get to come here, is it?'

'I would guess so,' said Brother Hamish carefully.

Croft decided to shift the questioning. 'There were three of you attending the symposium, weren't there?'

'That's right. We always send along what you might call a token force to these things, to show interest. Father Anselm suggested I might go along because I had worked at one time in a dockland settlement. Personally I find these things break my routine in a rather unfortunate way, but still, the discussions were most interesting.'

'And then there was – ' Croft consulted his list – 'Brother Jonathan. I'll talk to him, of course, but perhaps you could tell me what his reason was for attending.'

'I'm afraid you won't get a great deal out of talking to him,' said Brother Hamish. Why did Croft get the impression that there was a note of concern in his voice? 'He's very old, and – not to put too fine a point on it – nearly senile.'

'An odd choice, surely?'

'Not really, Inspector, when you understand our little Community.' Brother Hamish leaned forward, and his watery, restless eyes seemed to ooze sincerity. 'He is our oldest member, and greatly honoured by us all for that reason alone. He has been here more than forty years. In his time he has been a man with a very good brain. He was a schoolmaster at a highly respected school – very highly respected. Of course he is conscious that his brain is not what it was, but he does make very great efforts to keep contact with things. We thought it would please him to be asked to go along to the discussions. We thought it would make him feel useful and wanted.'

'I see. It sounds a very kindly idea. What about Brother Dominic, then?'

'Oh, it was natural that he should go along. He almost always did. He had the best brain of all of us – apart from Father Anselm, of course.'

'Ah, I see. Then he was clever.'

'Intelligent would be the word I'd use,' said Brother Hamish, with a darted glance from the floor to Croft.

'How did this – intelligence show itself? You seem to have so little contact with each other that I wonder on what basis you make a judgment of that kind.'

'That's very easy, Inspector,' said Brother Hamish. 'You will understand that we have all entirely renounced the world. When we do talk among ourselves it is almost entirely on spiritual matters. When we have crises, they are crises of belief, and in that case, of course we go to each other for help. In these circumstances one can judge immediately the quality of a man's intelligence. It is at such times that it shows. Brother Dominic's was formidable. In discussion there was no one to touch him. In quelling nagging doubts he had superb authority. The Community will miss him sadly.'

It was an impressive tribute. Was it the whole truth? Croft regretted that he continued to find Brother Hamish a less than impressive witness.

The evening at this time of year was usually the pleasantest time of day at St Botolph's, and in some ways the most beautiful. The heat of the scorching July days declined into a pleasant warmth, and the moors plumped themselves in the mellow evening light. It was one of those summers that doesn't happen in England, except in the romantic poets. After dinner that same evening Ernest Clayton – rather pleased, perhaps, that the Bishop now needed him less – took a brisk walk to the farthest limits of the walls, and then made his way back around but within them, thinking of the murder, and weighing the possibilities as to whether the symposium delegates or one of the members of the Community was to be considered the most likely murderer.

He went over in his mind the various members of the group. Who would have had the sheer nerve to do such a horrendous thing? Not the Bishop, surely? And would Philip Lambton? Of the others, all, probably, would possess the physical strength, granted Dominic was asleep when he was attacked. On the other hand, Randi Paulsen would have had to move the wardrobe from her door – hardly possible without being heard. Discarding her, he let his mind play over the other suspects, and from them to the anonymous mass of brothers.

As far as the physical set-up of the murder was concerned, he felt sure that the Inspector would consider the most likely culprit to be one of the group. On the other hand, psychologically it must surely seem more likely that the murderer was one of Brother Dominic's fellow monks. Contemplating this latter possibility, he put himself in the Inspector's shoes and asked himself a question: if one of the other brothers wanted to murder Brother Dominic, would he be most likely to do it at a time when the Community had guests in some number, or when the brothers were on their own? He came to the conclusion that if the murder was to come out into the open and be investigated in the normal way, it would be better to do it when there were guests. On the other hand, if it could be hushed up within the Community, then it would be better to do it when they were alone.

He immediately dismissed this last thought. The situation did not arise. The murder *had* been done when there were guests. He had no reason to accuse Father Anselm of being capable of hushing up a murder in the Community.

And yet he did think Father Anselm capable of hushing up a murder.

He remembered the Bishop's account of his conversation with Father Anselm on that terrifying night. He wondered why the more he thought of Father Anselm the less he –

And then he saw the figure again. Clayton was by now nearly back to the main building, and he had just turned a corner in the outside wall. Previously concealed, he could now be seen, and see. And between him and the large wooden barn stood the figure he had seen and been puzzled by the day before the murder. Here he was again, hooded, robed, sandalled.

For a few seconds he was speechless, and in that second the figure disappeared into the barn. Speeding his steps to a gentle run, Ernest Clayton rapidly gained the barn, and flung open the door. It took him some seconds for his eyes to accustom themselves to the gloom.

'I say,' he said feebly. Then he saw that directly opposite him was another door, and it was swinging on its hinges. He sped over and threw it open.

Two or three hundred yards away, speeding round the wall of the monks' dormitory wing like a dark angel, was his man. There was no chance of getting hold of him now. But that last glimpse had made Ernest Clayton quite sure who it was he had seen.

It was the corrupted cherub to whom he had given a lift in his car.

CHAPTER XII

GIRDING UP LOINS

AFTER COMPLINE Ernest Clayton and the Bishop got together, and talked late into the night. The subject admitted of an infinity of interpretations, and the Bishop seemed inclined to procrastinate. The first thing Clayton had to do was to convince him that something must be very wrong indeed at the Community of St Botolph's.

'But there is nothing intrinsically suspicious in a young man you knew in the outside world turning up as a monk here,' said the Bishop of Peckham with a sort of wheedle in his voice.

'You don't know the young man,' said Clayton. 'He has vile manners, foul language and an obscenely twisted mind.'

' "The wind bloweth where it listeth",' said the Bishop tentatively.

'The only thing blowing in this young sprig is a strong current of hot air,' said Clayton firmly.

'That's often the type who *do* get religion all of a sudden,' said the Bishop sadly. 'The Church is one of the last professions where people feel obliged to listen to your opinions, however boring and ludicrous they are, and I suppose that's why.'

'True in general,' said Clayton, 'but not at St Botolph's. If we are to believe Father Anselm, ninety per cent of the day is spent in silence, which wouldn't suit this little lad one bit. The point really is this : I gave this boy a lift when I was on my way up here. That was one day before I first saw him within the Community's walls. When I spoke to him he said nothing about coming here, though he was talking to a clergyman, and talking about religion (or what he imagines to be religion). He said he was coming to

Hickley, but no more than that. Whenever I have seen him here, he has immediately panicked and vanished. Why?'

The Bishop pondered. 'No reason suggests itself,' he said.

'He is dressed as an ordinary brother,' said Clayton, 'but I have never seen him eating with the rest.'

'You could be mistaken there,' said the Bishop. 'When they're all together they look like one indistinguishable mass of humanity. Like Chinese, you know, only one mustn't say so. It's only when you come to talk to them individually that you come to start noticing individual characteristics.'

'That's true,' said Clayton. 'Perhaps I should try to get a closer look at breakfast time. But even if he is with them, it won't alter the main point as I see it.'

'And – er – what is that?' asked the Bishop, plainly with a degree of apprehension.

'That there is more going on in this monastery than meets the eye.'

There was a silence of some seconds. The Bishop had known that Clayton must be thinking along these lines, and he was himself beginning to find some such conclusion irresistible. It was, nevertheless, as unwelcome a conclusion as could well be. He had already resigned himself to the fact that for some time to come he would be, in popular estimation, the Bishop involved in 'that murder case at the monastery'. He had, in fact, already settled it in his mind that it would be well for the present Archbishop not to resign at seventy, but to soldier on for a few years longer, so completely did he see his chances as having been ditched for the immediate future. But more pessimistic than this a cheery soul like the Bishop could not willingly be. And if, in addition to the murder, he were involved in the uncovering of something fishy at St Botolph's (and however pure his motives and however above reproach his conduct in the affair, his merely being involved would be enough for at least one of the newspapers for whom he was a *bête noire*) then he would be forced to say goodbye to his chances for ever. Even the headlines that would come to be written made him blush to the very lobes of his ears to think of. He was beginning to regret more and more the over-close relationship he had formed with Ernest Clayton since the murder. If only he had managed to stand on his own two feet.

'I see,' he said.

That's the first hurdle over, said Ernest Clayton to himself. Aloud he said: 'Of course this is part of a larger pattern. Tell me, do you completely trust Father Anselm?'

'I'm not in the habit of going around mistrusting people,' complained the Bishop, half-way between a whine and a bluster. 'He is the superior of this order, he was appointed by Leeds, and I don't go around expecting that people will turn out to be . . .' He expired into silence, and then he said: 'Well, no. I can't say I do.'

'Neither do I,' said Clayton firmly. 'So the next question is, what do we do?'

The answer that presented itself to the Bishop's mind was 'nothing', but he felt that it had to be skilfully wrapped up. 'The important thing,' he said, 'is to avoid scandal to the Church.'

He means 'do nothing', said Clayton to himself. Aloud he said: 'These days that's next to impossible. And more often than not trying to avoid scandal only brings it down in double quantity on your head. Think of Watergate.'

'I do not see that the cases are remotely comparable,' said the Bishop stiffly, obviously not relishing the implied comparison with the unfortunate Richard (at least he'd *had* the Presidency, he said to himself, and I never have).

'I don't intend any comparison,' said Clayton. 'I merely wanted to point to the difficulties involved in keeping the lid on a thing like this. Say there is something going on here. Say you get rid of three or four of the brothers, and perhaps shift Father Anselm. You sit back and thank your stars how easily the whole thing has sorted itself out. Then the brothers begin to talk. Have you noticed what terrible blabbermouths ex-nuns and monks are? They're worse

than de-frocked priests. And they seem to think that release
from their vows of silence releases them from any obligation
towards common sense too. Mark my words, once outside
these walls, they'd head like homing pigeons for Fleet
Street, and the next thing you knew, all the gory details
would be splashed on the front page of the *Sun*.'

The Bishop was beginning to think Clayton was a very
uncomfortable companion. Of course what he said was
true, but nobody likes having the comforting lies they have
fed themselves with dashed so brutally from their lips. 'The
important thing is to keep the Church's hands as clean as
possible,' he said.

'Amen to that,' said Clayton. 'Now, how do you suggest
we should proceed?'

'Well,' said the Bishop, very slowly, 'I suppose the best
first step would be to approach Father Anselm. Take him
aside and confront him with our suspicions.'

'And what if he simply denies there is anything out of
the ordinary going on?' asked Ernest Clayton, mentally
adding: And what if he manages to reduce you to a
quivering jelly as usual?

'That,' said the Bishop wrapping the shreds of his
dignity around him, 'will depend on the convincingness of
the denials. I'm sure you wouldn't wish to prejudge the
issue. We have to approach this thing in a completely calm
and judicious way. He may have a completely convincing
explanation for the presence and behaviour of this young
man.'

'Quite, quite,' said Ernest Clayton. 'And if he hasn't?'

By now the Bishop was finding Clayton distinctly over-
importunate. He ended the conversation almost brusquely.
'The thing we must try to avoid is a police investigation.
If they don't uncover anything in their murder enquiry,
then you can be quite sure it's no business of theirs. It's
Leeds's diocese, his pigeon. If Anselm's answers are unsatisfactory, I shall put the matter before Leeds, and leave
him to take what action he thinks fit.'

Getting well clear before the investigation starts, said Clayton to himself. He had a vision of the Bishop publicly washing his hands on Peckham Rye.

Inspector Croft looked at the knife. It was a strong, tough affair, mass-produced, but highly efficient. The lab boys had said it was of a type much used by the more serious type of fishermen. Not meant to be used on tiddlers, but on the bigger fish. There were no fingerprints on it, but the blood was of the same group as Brother Dominic's. There could be little doubt that he was the latest fish that this murderous little weapon had had to cope with.

Where had it come from, how had it come to hand? The knife used by the Bishop of Mitabezi on the unsuspecting lamb had come from High Table. It had been used for carving a joint of beef that evening, and the fingerprints of both bishops were on it. If Mitabezi had proceeded from human to animal sacrifice, he had been very much more circumspect about the human part of the operation. If it was one of the other delegates, or one of the brothers, where had they got the knife from? Had they brought it with them? Did the brothers fish? That seemed a possible line of enquiry. Not within the Community walls, that was certain, for there was no river or stream. Still, Croft knew they went outside now and then. And fishing did seem to him a peaceful, gentle occupation for a monk, though fish might not agree.

He shook his head. On the whole it seemed unlikely he would get anywhere with the knife. None of the delegates would admit bringing it. Would any of them have mentioned it in conversation before the murder? Hardly. If they had, they probably wouldn't have used it.

He got up, looked around Father Anselm's austere little study, and went out into the dark corridor. Here, perhaps, one of the brothers had lurked when Father Anselm had locked up for the night. He considered the idea quite dispassionately – it did not give him the shivers, as it had the

Bishop of Peckham. Probably the room where the symposium meetings were held was a more likely place. If, of course, Father Anselm had in fact locked up. The permutations of possibilities were endless. At any rate he was clear in his mind that the main part of the building offered sufficient scope for someone with iron nerve – and the injuries to Brother Dominic irresistibly suggested just such a person – to hide in, to await a suitable time to commit the deed. On the other hand, there was the question of the brothers' wing.

The entrance to this wing was down another short, dark corridor just off the main hall. It was sealed off from the main building by a heavy door with bars and bolts. Croft inspected the lock and the bolts. Both seemed to be in regular use. Once inside he was confronted by a steep flight of stairs. The ground floor of this wing, he had earlier ascertained, housed the heavier farming implements, with some modern equipment for repair work, and a car. There was no direct access from the upper storey. At the top of the stairway was a small landing, and leading off from it two dark corridors. The brothers' cells were on either side of these. They were all very small, smaller than Brother Dominic's, and they were furnished only with a bed, a hard chair, a rough shelf, and such devotional articles as the various brothers had brought to them – crucifixes mostly, and many statuettes of the Virgin Mary. By no means all the cells showed signs of habitation. All the outer ones were used : these were obviously preferable, having small windows, though they were above head level. Only a few of the inner ones were in use, and these had skylights which could just be opened by standing on a chair. Croft stood on one, hauled himself up to the frame, and peered out on to the roof : a fit man could no doubt get himself up there, but he would have to take a rope or knotted sheets to negotiate the drop. The outside rooms were somewhat easier, but only a smallish man could get through the windows (Croft couldn't see Brother Hamish doing it, for instance, since his figure was of the pear-drop variety, and in general he seemed too soft and flabby), and here too one would need some kind of rope to reach the ground.

Back in the main building Croft set Sergeant Forsyte and a couple of constables to inspect the windows and skylights for signs of human egress, but he was not hopeful. All things considered, he thought it more likely that if it was a member of the Community he was after, he had hidden in the main building.

But from a purely practical point of view he had to agree with the view of Father Anselm, that the most likely murderer would be one of those who slept in the main building. Which left one with the highly puzzling question of motive.

The next morning Clayton conducted his survey of the assembled brothers. He inspected as he went in those few who were already seated; he hid the spoon for his boiled egg, and went down to borrow one from a table where one of the brothers had seemed to bear a faint resemblance to the corrupted cherub (but his fair hair turned out to be pitifully thin, and his childish wire-rimmed glasses destroyed the idea at once) and at the end of the meal he walked slowly through the four tables of eating brothers with the Bishop of Peckham, the two of them deep in conversation about the phenomenon of geographical inertia. All in all Clayton got a good look at every man seated there.

Middle-aged men, with the light of faith in their eyes; young men, dulled, characterless; good-looking men with something of the dead brother's inhuman efficiency in their eyes and mouth; old men and soon-to-be-old men, looking like other old men in the outside world; sad faces; contented faces; cunning faces; bland faces; pimpled faces; bored, discontented, rebellious faces; behind the conformity of the coarse brown robes, what was to be seen? A cross-section of humanity. If you looked at the faces in a government department, you would see precisely the same things.

Deep in the nearly meaningless conversation, which had involved several stops for point-making and gesticulation, Clayton and the Bishop finally gained the shade of the little cloistered rooms off the main hall.

'He wasn't there,' said Clayton to the Bishop. 'We're going to have to confront Anselm.'

'They were rather obvious about it, didn't you think?' said one brother *sotto voce* to another.

Inspector Croft was on the phone to the Chief Constable. Sir Henry Abbotsford had taken a personal interest in the case since his dramatic phone call from the Bishop of Peckham. It seemed likely to provide a fertile topic of conversation (the word Sir Henry used to describe his holding forth) at future meetings of bodies whose committees Sir Henry graced. And the Chief Constable shared the universal human instinct to want to find out what goes on behind closed doors, whether those doors belong to a Whitehall department, a jail, a monastery, or Buckingham Palace.

'It's an odd case, in every possible way,' Croft was saying, with all the appearance of finding this phone call expendable. 'The idea of a random collection of people coming to a monastery and one of them bumping off one of the monks – it takes some swallowing.' He allowed Sir Henry a short interjection. 'Well, yes, bumping off one of the lambs is pretty way out too, but it's the human being that brought us on to the scene.'

'You do think it's one of the guests at the Community, then?' asked Sir Henry.

'As far as I can see, anyone here is a possibility. It would be easier for one of the guests to do it, or Father Anselm. Perhaps that's why I have this hunch that *if* it was one of the brothers, either he was in cahoots with Father Anselm, or Anselm has a good idea who did it. Just a hunch, no more. But there's no doubt about it, Anselm is an immensely impressive figure. And of course one would have to have a lot to go on before one started charging the head of a religious order with a crime like murder!'

'The main thing is, Croft,' said Sir Henry Abbotsford, 'be discreet. We can thank our lucky stars the Plunkett business seems to have been got over without the press getting on to it. But they've already begun to show a more than routine interest in the case. By tomorrow they may have descended on Hickley like a flock of vultures. That's why I say there must be absolute and complete discretion.'

'I quite understand, sir,' said Croft. 'As far as the press is concerned, the story is that I've been on the case from the beginning. And if I uncover anything nasty, I suppose I'm to keep the lid on it if I possibly can.'

'Exactly,' said Sir Henry. He added hopefully: '*Have* you uncovered anything nasty?'

'Not yet,' admitted Croft. 'Apart from the body, of course, which was not a pretty sight. Really I haven't got anywhere at all yet. And I feel I'll have to let all these visitors go on Saturday, or not too long afterwards. That was when they were due to go home anyway.'

'I suppose this symposium thing has gone by the board, has it?' asked Sir Henry.

'Oh, yes, completely collapsed. No regular sessions planned. They pray a bit, of course, but most of the time they seem to be mooning about and getting on each other's nerves. It's a bit of a laugh really. "The Role of the Church in the Modern World" they called this do. I'm afraid in the event they've found the modern world has been too much with them.'

'Anyway, you're letting them go, are you?'

'Yes, I feel I have to. But in the meanwhile I'm trying to get reports from their local police on them – as many details as possible on their backgrounds, careers, marriages – all the local gossip, in fact.'

'It should make good reading,' said Sir Henry.

'Do you really think so?' asked Croft dubiously. 'And of course I'm finding out what I can about the victim. I

have a few basics – name, address, school and so on. There
are no near relatives, I understand, but I should be able
to find someone who knew him outside. Of course there is
no police record on him.'

'But remember, above all be discreet,' said Sir Henry.

'You can count on me,' said Croft, hanging up.

But how *could* one be discreet about a police investigation of the private lives of a collection of churchmen, two
of them bishops and two of them women? It would be the
talk of the various parishes and dioceses for months. And
if the case wasn't solved, there was going to be a lot of dirt
left around – clinging, one might say, to the whited sepul-
chres.

CHAPTER XIII

CONFRONTATION

THE ATMOSPHERE WAS definitely deteriorating. Since the departure of Plunkett the delegates had somehow been less willing to talk about the murder investigation and the questions Inspector Croft had put to them. Since the maniac had been taken off, things had somehow become more real.

They had therefore been forced back as a topic of conversation on religion – hardly a subject to bring out the best in anyone. As they lounged around the lawn after breakfast Philip Lambton probed Randi Paulsen on her attitude to drink, dancing, ritual, and a whole range of subjects on which the Anglican Church would claim to have liberalized its attitudes over the last century. Randi's replies, replete with the sourest kind of smug bigotry (and accompanied by the fearsome smile), were not to his liking.

'It's like Cromwell's England!' he said. 'I didn't realize there were still churches like that outside the nutty-fringe groups. And to think of them existing in Scandinavia!'

'At least we understand that our job is to spread the gospel,' snapped back Randi Paulsen, viciously flicking at the switch of her smile, 'and not to run a second-rate variety agency.'

Watching the exchange, and almost purring with pleasure, was Bente Frøystad.

'I get the impression,' said Ernest Clayton to her, 'that you are not a great admirer of your fellow churchwoman.'

Bente Frøystad shrugged and grinned. 'We get on, because we have to. There are only a handful of ordained women in Norway, so inevitably we see each other a fair bit. And for the immediate future, I have to travel back with her. You know, she's what in your terms I suppose should be called very low church. We have something of the same sort of divisions in our church too. Therefore she does not approve of me – she thinks I'm much too high, and progressive, and ceremonial, and permissive and all that sort of thing. She keeps trying to drive me into a corner and make me confess I'm in favour of abortion on demand. She has a desperate need of something to tut-tut about. Actually I'm *not* in favour of it, but I'm certainly not going to tell her that. She's really very stupid – and a vicious little prig to boot.'

Not a bad summing up, thought Ernest Clayton, though certainly not a kind one. He turned to the Bishop of Peckham, who was feigning deep interest in a conversation with Simeon P. Fleishman and trying not to catch his eye.

'Perhaps it's time we went to look for Father Anselm,' said Clayton taking his arm.

'Oh – do you think so? Isn't it rather early?'

'No – it's ten o'clock.'

'I suppose not, no. Where will he be, do you think? Now he no longer has an office.'

'We'll find him,' said Ernest Clayton determinedly.

Oddly enough the first background report to get through to Inspector Croft was one of the foreign ones. Dictated to the Leeds police from the police station in Bergen, it was the report on Randi Paulsen. It was written by the local *lensman*, the sheriff of her little parish, and had been translated in Bergen.

'Randi Paulsen has been at Svartøy now during one and a half year,' the report ran. 'At first was many unwilling to have woman priest, and it was much opposition. However, since coming has such opinions changed. Miss Paulsen is a very active and enthusiastic leader of Christian activity in the community. She has under-taken many new projects, and her preachings and her teachings are very popular. She also does much visiting with the sick and the older peoples. She has fought strongly against the looser element in the community and has in this way done much good works particularly against alcohol misuses and sexual things. Speaking as a practising Christian I would say that Miss Paulsen has transformed Svartøy in her time here, and it is impossible to think of her in connection with police investigation.'

Croft got on the phone to Leeds.

'Get on to Norway again,' he said, 'and tell them I'd like a report on Randi Paulsen written by someone who is *not* a practising Christian.'

Father Anselm was not too difficult to find. He had been informed of the all-too-obvious inspection by Clayton and the Bishop of Peckham of the brothers at their breakfast. He was therefore half expecting a visit. The two found him in the chapel at prayer. Unwilling, of course, to interrupt him, they stood by the door. Though he was kneeling in the back row of seats, Father Anselm was quite oblivious of their presence. He went on praying for a very, very long time. Finally, after several sessions of extra time, he rose, saw Clayton and the Bishop in the doorway, raised his eyebrows and came forward.

'Is there anything I can do?' he asked, fixing his keen, intimidating gaze on one after the other.

'Yes – we should rather like to have a few words with you,' said Ernest Clayton. Father Anselm gestured to him, as if to say, 'Go right ahead.' But Clayton was not having that. 'Somewhere more private would be better – if there *is* anywhere.' Suppressing a spasm of irritation which flitted over his mouth revealingly, Father Anselm led the way through the murky corridors to the conference room. Once inside, he turned, drew a bunch of keys from a rope around his waist, and locked the door. He turned, gave the two another piercing look, as if to say, 'Is this private enough for you?', and gestured them towards the easy chairs. What surprised Clayton was that, unusually for him, he consented to sit down in one himself. He sat, in fact, in a perfectly relaxed manner, obviously aware that his height gave him a perceptible advantage over the other two. He looked full of calm confidence.

'Now, again, what can I do for you?' he asked.

Ernest Clayton had already decided that it would be he who did the talking.

'I'll come to the point at once,' he said. 'Yesterday I saw a young man within the walls here, dressed as one of your brothers. He was a young man – boy, perhaps, would be a better description – whom I'd met before. I gave him a lift in my car up here, and he impressed me very disagreeably. In fact, I was forced to turn him out. He was obsessed with sex, ill-mannered, and foul in his language. To my mind he was very obviously the delinquent type, and he seemed to be making an effort to disgust me and shock me. You will see, I think, why I was disturbed to find him among your brothers here.'

Father Anselm had been regarding him with something close to an amiable smile on his face. Clayton wondered what that unprecedented aspect could portend. When he finished speaking, Father Anselm left a couple of seconds' silence, and then said: 'Yes, I can see why you were disturbed.' There was a slight stress on the 'you'. Father Anselm said no more, merely continuing to look blandly on his inquisitor.

'Could you explain, then,' said Ernest Clayton, rather put off his stride, 'how this young man came to be here?'

'No, I could not,' said Father Anselm equably. 'Even if I knew who you were referring to, and even if I knew why he was here, I would not do so. It is my invariable custom never to discuss the private affairs of either the brothers who have taken their vows, or the occasional guests here. To do so would be an unforgivable breach of trust.'

'I see,' said Ernest Clayton. 'I should explain that both

times I have seen him within the Community's walls he has avoided me, disappeared suddenly – on one occasion running very fast to avoid being questioned. You can hardly wonder if I am suspicious.'

'No, no,' said Father Anselm genially, 'I am not in the least surprised at your being suspicious.' He left another long pause, which Ernest Clayton realized was designed to give him time to realize what a silly little boy he was being. 'On the other hand,' went on Father Anselm, 'an intelligent mind would, I think, remember that our brothers come here to get away from the world. Many are most loath to come into contact with people from outside the walls – particularly brothers who have recently joined the Community, and particularly if the person from the outside world was known to them in their private life. Such behaviour is quite normal, I assure you.'

'Not *running away,* surely?'

'Yes, surely. You have an image in your mind of a monk : a serious, pious, grave young man. Running does not fit neatly into your image, and therefore you can't imagine a monk running away. But that is only one kind – perhaps quite a small number. There are many other kinds : frightened men, disturbed men, and they will act in many different ways that you would find quite impossible to make conform to your stereotype, and you will be surprised. But you must not expect *me* to be surprised. I know all the kinds.'

Thus far, Ernest Clayton had to admit, Father Anselm was doing rather well. He himself was in the unfortunate position that the more he brought his suspicions and the reasons for them out in the open, the more flimsy they appeared. But once he had waded in, there seemed no alternative but to swim out to sea.

'That isn't quite the only thing that has worried me,' he went on, looking straight into Father Anselm's bland but cold blue eyes. 'When the murder was discovered, you tried to persuade the Bishop here that the murderer must be one of our group in the guest wing, one of the delegates to the symposium, even though on a factual level the argument wouldn't hold water for a moment.'

Father Anselm shrugged, and his eyes looked straight back at Ernest Clayton without the slightest degree of embarrassment. 'It was an opinion. It is still my opinion. I am not a detective, and therefore my opinions are quite open to correction or disagreement.'

'You are not a detective, of course. On the other hand, you are not a fool either.'

'I am grateful for your excellent opinion.' Father Anselm stirred a little in his chair, as he prepared to shift his stance and go on to the attack. 'And not being a fool I am of course quite aware of the direction in which all these questions are leading. How is one to put it? I gather you find something "fishy" in our little Community. I do not know what you suspect, or even whether you have got as far as to suspect anything specific. But I must say that your reasons for suspicion seem extraordinarily flimsy, or else based on sheer ignorance of such a community as this and the kind of people who join it. That being so, your suspicions are of no interest to me. Until you give me some concrete reason for them, I do not feel called upon to give you any further explanations.'

He had shown no anger : on the contrary, no equanimity could be more complete than his. Ernest Clayton decided he must be even more brutal, in an attempt to flush him out.

'You tried to suggest to the Bishop after the murder that the whole thing could be hushed up,' he said baldly.

Father Anselm looked benevolently astonished. 'Is that the impression you gained?' he said, turning to the Bishop. 'How very extraordinary. And what exactly was it I said that made you think I was suggesting such a very improper course?'

The Bishop gulped and flapped his hands nervously. He had been pessimistic about this meeting to start with, and it was very clear to him by now which way it was going. 'Well, it wasn't exactly what you *said*,' he muttered feebly, 'it was more that this was . . . this seemed . . . seemed to be an idea that was in the air.'

Father Anselm managed an exquisitely timed pause. 'I see,' he said. Then after another pause for meditation, and turning towards Ernest Clayton, he said : 'And what else am I to be accountable for ?'

Ernest Clayton had a general feeling of having been badly routed. 'I'm quite willing to admit,' he said, 'that many of the things that have given me the idea that – that things are not quite as they should be, are very small things, insignificant in themselves. Nevertheless, a murder is not insignificant. Inevitably I can't quite divorce in my mind these small things from this one big thing, and I suppose the police would feel the same way. I'm quite sure, for instance, that they would be anxious to follow up all possible causes of suspicion, simply because they could be relevant to the murder.'

Father Anselm raised his eyebrows and said nothing.

'Now the thing that really worries me,' went on Clayton, 'is the young man appearing here. And if you are not willing to explain how that could come about, I am quite willing to turn the matter over to them, and trust to their judgement of how far it is significant.'

There was a fluttering gesture of protest from the Bishop of Peckham, and it was not lost on Father Anselm. It occurred to him that the Bishop was more of an ally than an opponent, and that a degree of compromise might well be on the cards.

'Of course, that is as you decide, Mr Clayton,' he said courteously, 'since the whole notion is apparently yours. I need hardly say that everything in the Community is open to inspection, whether by our regular visitor, by the Church authorities or by the police. My only reason for preferring the Church to the police is the sort of publicity which inevitably seems to attend on police enquiries these days. It is bad enough to have the murder investigation on our hands, but if it can be contained to that, not too much harm need be done. But a general investigation, by the police, of the Community as a whole could hardly be good for the Church generally. Perhaps you, My Lord, might agree with me on that point, at any rate.'

'Oh – er – absolutely, quite. Very regrettable, absolutely to be avoided,' stammered the Bishop with an agonized expression on his face. 'The very last thing we want.'

'I wonder if I may say a few things about the people who come here,' said Father Anselm, still as benign and inscrutable as he had been throughout the interview, 'talking, please understand, in general and not in particular. I emphasize this, because the one thing which I can not tolerate is the suggestion that I could betray the trust of anyone who has come here in distress. Would you allow me?'

'Do, do – please,' burbled the Bishop.

'As I implied, there are many types who come here with the notion that they may have a vocation for the religious life. Many of them are young people. You are no doubt as aware as any of the thirst for religion – almost *any* religion, it sometimes seems – among the young today. It has, I believe, formed the subject for many a sermon and homily among my brothers in the clergy.'

He looked at Ernest Clayton, who nodded – not to agree with the existence of such a thirst, merely to agree that it was a frequent topic for sermonizing.

'This thirst leads many people to us. Many, most, are quite unsuited to the life. Some are leading lives in the world that are, to the Church's thinking, misguided, even scandalous. I don't know if you feel that we should reject sinners?' He smiled benignly at Clayton. 'Turn them out of our car, so to speak. We feel we cannot. We feel that to reject them would be a negation of the whole Christian message, which was a message to sinners. So if, when we have talked to them, and explained to them what the life here entails, they still feel they want to join us for a short time, as an experiment, then we allow them to do so. And in more than one case this short time has become a longer time, and the man has finally taken his vows, joined us, to devote his life to our ideals. To me, with I hope pardonable pride, this seems something of a triumph. But if, as very frequently happens, the person is quite unsuited to our life, he finds it out very soon, and leaves us. No harm has been done. Perhaps, in the long run, some good has been, a grain has been sown : who can tell? But that is our policy, and I hope it explains some of the things that have bewildered you.'

He sat back, with a degree of benevolent self-satisfaction. He was rewarded by the Bishop saying: 'Yes, indeed. A most interesting statement. A very commendable policy.'

'I am still not really happy in my mind about why the young man should be so scared of me as to run away,' said Ernest Clayton.

'I have suggested one possible reason. That you represent in his mind the world he is trying to run away from. Another presents itself : if he had behaved badly to you, he may well have been overcome by feelings of shame. You smile, but I cannot think that quite so improbable as you seem to. I have seen the spiritual atmosphere of the Community work great changes on people in a very short space of time.'

'In this case,' said Ernest Clayton, 'you seem to have been so convinced by the quick-working influence of the Community that you let him don the habit of a brother of the Community almost as soon as he arrived,' said Ernest Clayton. 'I wonder whether you were not perhaps a little too easily convinced. Or is that the usual practice?'

'Not the usual practice, no. Not unless it was, as you say, someone who we were very certain had a vocation.'

'And you did feel that in this case?'

'You forget, I am not talking about particular cases,' said Father Anselm reprovingly. 'And you forget too that the guest wing was occupied by members of the symposium.'

'There are spare rooms there.'

'It seemed undesirable to disturb the group with an alien element. And above all I was unwilling to put him in among you due to the presence in the group of – women.'

It seemed an excellent argument, even if the last word was brought out with an expression akin to distaste. Ernest Clayton was very close to defeat, but he tried one last throw.

'All this seems very satisfactory,' he said. 'I confess you have laid some of my fears to rest. I wonder if you could persuade the young man to have a few words with me, just to confirm matters. Then we can let the thing drop entirely.'

'That I'm afraid would be impossible. In this case the experiment proved – *not* a success.'

'He has left? Already?'

Father Anselm cast a glance less benign than his recent ones at Ernest Clayton. 'I have no doubt it was your doing. He felt pursued, spied on.'

'I see,' said Clayton. 'Very regrettable, no doubt. I trust I shall have done no permanent harm, if he has a genuine vocation for the religious life. Did you think he had such a vocation, by the way?'

'It would be presumptuous of me to give an opinion,' said Father Anselm gravely. 'Such decisions are not to be taken lightly. And now, if you have finished – '

He ushered them to the door and unlocked it. Both men, safely on the other side of the door, felt very like naughty schoolboys who had avoided a wigging but had been given a talking down which was almost worse. And Clayton was alarmed to see that the Bishop showed signs of a resolve never, under any circumstances, to be a naughty boy again.

CHAPTER XIV

SCENES FROM CLERICAL LIFE

'THE KNIFE, unfortunately, tells us nothing,' said Detective-Inspector Croft regretfully to Sergeant Forsyte, looking down at the sturdy, razor-sharp instrument that had been discovered through Inspector Plunkett's zeal. 'They are a standard type, and can be bought anywhere – including Norway, no doubt.'

'Where did it come from? Had they anything of the sort in the Community?' asked Forsyte.

'Father Anselm says that none of the monks fished. He says he has never seen anything of the sort around.'

'You don't believe him?' asked Forsyte, unsure whether he had caught a note of scepticism in Croft's voice.

'It's not our business to believe people, unless there's some evidence to back up what they say,' said Croft, 'even if they wear flowing robes and swing rosaries. For what it's worth, I certainly find Anselm enormously impressive. But I believe in paying less attention to impressions, and more to facts. One thing that puzzles me about the set-up of the murder is what the murderer wore, and that's what I'm thinking about as of now.'

'What he wore?'

'There was blood, plenty of it. Some of it must have got on the murderer. Think of how the thing was done: it couldn't have been easy, even if Brother Dominic was sleeping, which presumably he was. I'd guess whoever it was held something over his mouth while he slit him open – not easy, as I say, and needing a fair amount of strength, whether natural or summoned up for the occasion from some kind of frenzy of hatred or whatever. Now, he was bound to get blood on him, whoever it was. What was he wearing, and where is it?'

'Nothing's been found in the search,' said Forsyte.

'No. But searching a huge area like this and not quite knowing what you are after is a nightmare game. I wonder if they're looking in the right places. It seems to me the two alternatives were to clean it or to destroy it, whatever it was. I want particular attention paid to the laundry, and to any stoves or fires there may be.'

'I'll get the message through to the boys,' said Sergeant Forsyte. 'Anything else?'

'No. I'm going through all this background stuff. Just keep an eye on the delegates – overhear anything you can. It's them I'm interested in at the moment.'

'They're not talking much these days,' said Sergeant Forsyte, 'not when I'm near, anyway. While Plunkett was around I think they regarded me as a possible ally against him –'

'Rightly, I hope?' said Croft.

' – for the credit of the force,' continued Sergeant Forsyte imperturbably. 'But since then they've rather fallen apart, there being nothing to unite against, and I think they're all getting suspicious of each other, and of me too.'

'All to the good,' said Croft. 'A flaming row among them could be really interesting. Couldn't you ask them some really knotty theological questions, now, just to get them going?'

'I've never been greatly interested in religion, sir, not since the war,' said Forsyte gravely. 'But if you yourself would care to suggest a query I would do my best to make it sound convincing.'

Left to himself Croft sat back and studied the reports on the various delegates to the St Botolph's symposium. The reports in so far gave him little specific help, however revealing they might be of the state of the delegates' various churches. The saddest figure seemed to be Philip Lambton. He had been brought up in Lancaster by a widowed mother of strong will and ferocious gentility. Mrs Lambton was a tireless organizer of bazaars, secretary and one-time president of the Mothers' Union, feared bully of the local clergy, and one who kept her name before the Bishop by a series of long epistles on matters theological, organizational and frankly scandalous. Over-protected and over-driven, Philip had drifted through the most interesting decades of life in a state of severe atrophy of the will. He was ferociously bullied at school, gently bullied at university, mildly ridiculed in his first curacy. Through it all his devotion to his domineering mother had remained un-dimmed. 'I thought he'd have to break out somehow,' said a neighbour, who had had no love for the late Mrs Lamb-ton, 'but he never did.'

After her death by cancer Philip Lambton had gone to Liverpool, and before long he had shown signs of the 'breaking out' that the neighbour had predicted. The natural inclination of his congregation was to make their vicar into a much-petted son, for they were almost all female and over fifty. But Philip Lambton had shown a surprising tenacity in wriggling out of their blameless maternal embraces. In fact, he had begun to frequent coffee-bars and discotheques, and soon he was even wearing strange gear, riding a motor-bike around at high speed, and was heard to utter a weird jargon which was part genuine teenage argot, part a cod language fed to him by his new companions to see how far his gullibility would take him. In fact, he gradually delivered himself body and soul to the local exponents of pop culture, and he did it in the full glare of local publicity in which he did not detect the undertones of ridicule, though everyone else did. The new freedom, however, turned out to be not so very different from the old servitude.

'They just walk over him,' said a fellow clergyman who had tried to give him advice, but had found him too be-sotted by youth and publicity to listen. 'They borrow from him, swear at him, work him over, and still he comes back for more. I keep thinking he'll have to break out, but he never does.'

Stewart Phipps was a very different figure. Born to a London suburban family of civil servants, one with no strong religious affiliations, he had been little loved by his fellow grammar-school boys, on account of his harsh, fluent tongue. Even the teachers were very wary of his withering retorts, especially as he was indubitably bright. He passed his 'O' levels with flying colours, and everyone said it was just what they expected. They all added that they hoped it wouldn't go to his head.

And then something happened that his teachers were familiar enough with but which was extremely disconcerting and wounding to the boy himself. Mentally, he did not continue to expand. He had 'reached his top'. Of course the situation did not present itself quite like that to Phipps himself, but even he could not fail to notice that lesser, despised boys overtook him, boys he had browbeaten and withered. Even before he took his 'O' levels he had thought long and seriously about Oxbridge, had wavered between the two, had done some elementary research into the colleges and thought seriously which of them he would aim at. But when the time came he failed to get into either university.

His temper was not softened by disappointment. On the contrary, his scorn was still as readily on tap, but it was less effective, less feared, because it seemed to his fellows that it now had no solid basis in intellectual supremacy. Stewart Phipps had been deposed. A life of subordination and mediocrity seemed to yawn before his eyes. He decided to go into the Church.

It wasn't a quick decision. He had been interested in religion for some time, for its ritual had appealed to some suppressed sense of drama in him, and he grasped at anything that could seem to mark him off from 'the rest'. Stewart Phipps's religion was always of the sort that excluded others, and sought for reasons to exclude still more.

Once the decision was made, the Church was embraced whole-heartedly. It was the mid-sixties : left-wing radicalism was in the air. This too, in its most excluding version, was crushed to Stewart Phipps's lean, crusading breast, There was little room left for other enthusiasms, but he picked up a little wife and children around this time. Since no one to speak of went any longer to his church, what gossip the local Blackburn police had been able to pick up was from his neighbours – a hymn of hate which centred on his treatment of his dependants.

'He treats them like dirt beneath his feet,' said the next-door neighbour. 'It's not what I call Christianity, I know that. Shouts at her, sneers at her – well, go and look at her. She hasn't got an ounce of life left in her, and she was a pretty little thing before they married. Works her to death, that's what he does. And the little girls – well! he hardly says hello to them in the mornings, and it's my belief they hate him, young as they are.'

Two different types. Two murderers? Divorcing consideration of them from the fact of their ordination, Croft felt that both were possibilities, given the right circumstances. What was lacking was any idea why the encounter with Brother Dominic might have provided 'the right circumstances'.

The other two British clergy were less contemporary types. Ernest Clayton, who Croft had noticed early in his investigations and had found interesting to interview, had been twenty years in his little Lincolnshire parish, and was well-known and liked. This had not stopped church attendance declining, dribble by dribble. 'Of course, he made efforts, early on,' said one of his church wardens, 'but he seemed to lose heart. What can you do, after all? It's the same all over, isn't it?' He was on good terms with his daughters – two of them grown up and married, and one of them living in the nearest big town – but his wife was not altogether popular in the village. 'She's a real lady,' said one of the little congregation, 'and you don't see many of those these days. Still, it doesn't do, if you haven't got the means to keep it up. No good being snooty if your shoes let in water.' Croft guessed that Mrs Clayton had accustomed herself less easily than her husband to the reduced status of a clergyman's family in modern Britain.

The Bishop of Peckham, widowed, cosseted by his house-keeper, fond of his stomach and fond of his little joke, had at this stage of his earthly pilgrimage very little private life : his routine centred on his writing, his television appearances, his episcopal duties. He was popular with his staff, who put it over him in little things, thieved from him in lesser, forgivable ways, and kept the more unpleasant aspects of life – reporters, gushing women, quarrelsome clergymen and telephoning maniacs – out of his hair and away from his notice. They had nothing unpleasant to say about him, and clearly had no difficulty in managing him. Snoop as they might, the police of Peckham had been un-able to pick up any unsavoury gossip about him : no undue interest in the members of confirmation classes, of either sex; no hanging around public lavatories; no sudden urges to clean up Soho. His daring was of an entirely theological kind.

Two apparently good and well-adjusted men. Murderers? Well, Clayton looked as if he had the intelligence and the will. But what circumstances would be strong enough to make him kill? The Bishop had the intelligence, but surely not the will. It suddenly struck Croft as slightly comic that he should be considering a bishop as a possible murderer : the whole set-up led one into such bizarre speculations. Or was it so bizarre? It was a cliché of popular criminology that many murderers looked like bishops. That was why the first great disappointment of an English adolescent was usually the Chamber of Horrors at Madame Tussaud's. And Croft had known plenty of murderers who not only looked but for ninety per cent of the time behaved like bishops. Was the Bishop of Peckham a ninety-per-cent bishop?

He was interrupted in his speculations by Sergeant Forsyte, who came in hot and bothered.

'I think you'd better come and look at this,' he said. 'It
might be nothing, but I've sent for the technical boys.'

Croft followed Forsyte through the dim corridors, across
the Great Hall, and out into the twilight. In the centre of
the kitchen garden, only a few yards from the main door,
he saw a cluster of his own men, and went over to it.

'What is it?' he asked, and the policemen fanned out to
let him come in closer.

They were standing round an ancient incinerator, of
sturdy local iron-work, looking as old as the buildings themselves, and hidden from the general gaze behind a row of
green beans. It was capacious, and obviously used to destroy
garden rubbish. The fire had been doused, however, and
now the door was held open by one of the police boffins.
He beckoned Croft over.

'See here,' he said. Croft bent down close. Caught in the
hinge of the door were several long strands of material,
making up a little rectangle. As far as could be seen the
material, which was brown, was stained and discoloured in
some way.

'That's what your man was wearing, I'd say, wouldn't
you?' said the boffin.

'A monk's habit?' said Croft.

'Looks like it, doesn't it? That should make things
simpler for you, shouldn't it?'

Ernest Clayton was a good sleeper. He lived a contented
life, his job presented him with few problems that could
not be sloughed off at the end of the day, and his digestion
was good, never having been ruined by the sort of food and
drink which were well beyond his income. He slept, if not
the sleep of the just, at least the sleep of the temperate.

But tonight he did not sleep. When he did doze off, it
was fitful and troubled, and soon he was awake again,
staring at the ceiling, making patterns of the shadow cast

by the moon over his room, and trying to sort out his suspicions and see clearly his moral duties. All these considerations seemed to point in different directions.

One thing had become clear to him since his interview with Father Anselm that morning : his suspicions of that gentleman rested on laughably slight foundations. To that extent Anselm's points had gone home. On the other hand, suspicious of him he still was.

The simplest solution would be to go to the police. After all, it was undeniable that on the night of the murder, there was among the brothers an outsider, whose presence had not been declared to the police, and who had since left. He had no doubt that Detective-Inspector Croft would be more than interested to learn this.

On the other hand, he had hoped to be a little further than this when he presented the results of his investigations to the police. He had to admit to himself that since the Bishop had told him of the murder there had been gaining living space in his mind this image of himself handing the answer on a plate to the police, or at the very least asking the illuminating question that everybody else had forgotten to ask.

And then there was his loyalty to his church. Despondent though he was about the future of his religion, pessimistic though he was about the state of his church and (especially) the quality of its leadership, nevertheless it was to this church he had given his life, and this church that had provided him with his livelihood. It was undoubtedly true that if there was something untoward going on at St Botolph's it would be best for the Church if the matter were investigated by the Church. It wasn't only the Bishop of Peckham who felt that. But what sort of investigation would the Church undertake, and would its main aim be the fearless eliciting of the whole truth? Ernest Clayton wanted to think so, but he couldn't quite do so. He felt twinges of loyalty, conflicts of judgement. He also felt hot and sticky.

Finally he got up. His bed clung to him and oppressed him, as did the smallness of his room. He walked up and down, still going around in the same intellectual circles. Today he had been worsted by Father Anselm, well and truly. How was he to turn the tables? As he walked and thought, the first light of dawn began to creep in by the window of his room.

In the middle of his walk he heard a sound. It was very slight, and came, he judged, from the wall under his window, but farther along. Strange : there was no door in that wall, yet this had sounded like a door swinging open. The door to the main hall was round the corner, and surely too far away for him to hear.

He crept to the window and gently pushed aside the grey-green folk-weave curtain. He still could not see what had made the noise, but he could see two robed figures, walking away from the main building, past the barn whose side was visible to Ernest Clayton, and away towards the boundary wall. They walked steadily and determinedly – not hurrying, yet nearly so. When they reached the wall the taller of the two cupped his hands to make a stirrup, and the other, bundling his habit about him rather awkwardly, stepped into it, scrambled on to the top of the wall, and dropped over on to the ground on the other side.

The early morning light was still very dim, but Ernest Clayton was quite clear about what he saw next. First a brown monk's habit was thrown over the wall, and caught by the tall figure still inside. Then there was to be seen, scurrying away over the moors, a figure in jeans and white tee-shirt, fixing a ruck-sack clumsily on to his shoulders as he ran along. By this time the other figure, plainly intent on regaining the main building as quickly as possible, was in the shadow of the big barn. As he neared the main building, however, the morning light enabled the Reverend Clayton to be quite sure about his identity.

It was Father Anselm, and he had been escorting from the grounds of St Botolph's the corrupted cherub.

CHAPTER XV

FATHER CONFESSOR

THE WALL BENEATH the guest wing looked solid enough. The whole of St Botolph's bespoke Edwardian substantiality, transmuted into religious terms. Viewed from a distance there was no sign of skimping or faking in that one wall.

But when Ernest Clayton came closer, jaded but eager in the hot morning sun, he saw that – symbolic of St Botolph's as a whole? – all was not quite as it seemed. At one point towards the end of the wing, surrounded by tomato beds and an unlikely place for a casual visitor to stray in, the inquisitive eye could detect a regular rift in the brick, forming the shape of a small door. The conclusion seemed inevitable: the brick at this point must in fact be merely a thin imitation of the brick in the rest of the wall, and must swing open to admit people, or to allow the exit of people, who did not wish to use the main door.

To which room, or from which room? The geography of the inside of the building was difficult, particularly at this point, where the main hall had degenerated first into the little rooms where they had met on the first night for drinks, and then into the maze of corridors, bedrooms and discussion rooms. Ernest Clayton crinkled his brow. It could not be into Father Anselm's study – that was farther along. Could it be Brother Dominic's bedroom? Or perhaps the next bedroom along the corridor, which he knew to be Father Anselm's.

He turned, and found Father Anselm watching him.

There was nothing to do now but to have it out with him. He walked slowly towards the barn where Father Anselm was standing. From a distance he resembled a statue, quite immovable. Closer up Ernest Clayton wondered whether he was not more than a little taken aback.

'You have found our priest-hole, I see,' said Father Anselm, with a somewhat shaky urbanity.

'Is that what you call it?' said Ernest Clayton. 'Used these days for priests of pop culture, I believe?'

There was a pause. Ernest Clayton suspected this blow was not unanticipated. Finally Father Anselm nodded his head.

'I see. I rather thought I must have been detected.' Something of his old grimness of manner returned. 'You were spying on me last night,' he said, sourly accusing.

'I was looking out of my window,' said Ernest Clayton, with the calm that comes from knowing one holds high trumps.

'I see,' said Anselm deliberately. He turned his eyes towards the purple waves of moorland, stretching to the far walls and beyond, as if he were surveying his past life before bidding farewell to it forever. 'I think perhaps the time has come to take you into my confidence.'

'You mean to start telling the truth, I suppose,' said the Reverend Clayton. 'Is there any point? Clearly I must go to the police. You can save your explanation for them.'

'You imply that I have been lying,' said Father Anselm, who was certainly showing no signs of shame. 'I think you might regret that. At worst I have been – shall we say a trifle Jesuitical? I have never believed it wise to blurt out the whole truth, on every occasion. I have done no worse than occasionally withholding the full explanation from you and the Bishop.'

'Nonsense. You said the young man had left.'

'*You* said he had left. I refrained from correcting you. But it is foolish to quarrel about quibbles of that sort. I think you and the Bishop would be wise to hear the whole story and judge for yourselves. Shall we say in the conference room, in an hour's time?'

Father Anselm's air was brisk and confident. Ernest Clayton felt sorely torn. The involvement of the Bishop was

clearly a clever ploy on Father Anselm's part : he was confident he would prove putty in his hands. On the other
hand, it was not altogether an unfair ploy : he himself
had been careful to involve the Bishop earlier when making
his accusations, to add weight (or at any rate status) to his
mission. And then, Father Anselm's apparent confidence
did affect Clayton. It led him to consider the possibility
that, far from solving the murder, he might merely make
a fool of himself to the police. There is nothing more ridiculous than the amateur detective who fancies himself
Sherlock Holmes and turns out to be Watson.

And then, most potent of all was the itch of curiosity :
Ernest Clayton did desperately want to know the truth
about St Botolph's.

'I agree,' he said. 'In an hour's time.'

It was odd, thought Croft, that the least vivid report he
received was the collection of data on the victim. He had
from the beginning decided that the late Brother Dominic
was probably asking to be murdered, and it was his experience that in such cases the personality of the dead person
was usually much more interesting than the personality of
the murderer (as a bad smell is more interesting than a
deodorizing spray). But if this was the whole truth about
Brother Dominic, or Denis Crowther, it was a very dull
truth indeed : nothing came off the page to enable him
to pin down the nature of the man.

He had lived with his parents in Little Purlock, a village
near Chelmsford, and had gone to a minor public school
with an ecclesiastical tradition. His school-masters spoke of
his strong personality, the dominating influence he had over
other boys. He was clever, good at games, never in any
serious trouble. He did not mix widely on vacations at
home, and people spoke of him as remote and rather forbidding. His parents were the modern squire-equivalents :
his father had been early in the public-relations game, and
had built up a tidy fortune in the fifties. He and his wife

had glad-handed it around the village (the house they lived in had been the manor, and the owner had sold it to go and decay in warmth and comfort on the Algarve), but Denis Crowther had not been interested in playing the young squire. His parents were killed in a plane crash in Yugoslavia when he was nineteen. He had been left reasonably well-off. He kept the house in Little Purlock, but was only there at weekends, as he was working in some junior capacity with a City firm, and kept a flat in London. The first the villagers had heard of his entering the Community of St Botolph's was some months after he had ceased coming there, when the house was put up for sale.

There were two curious things about the report. It seemed that neither Denis Crowther nor his parents were regular church-goers – Easter communicants at best. Nor, in spite of the traditions of his school, was he remembered there as evincing any adolescent fervours in the matter of religion. It would seem, then, that his discovery of his vocation must have been the result of a sudden conversion. The other oddity was that the police could discover no trace of the activities in the City that the villagers spoke of. Investigations were continuing.

This last fact especially intrigued Croft : why should there be any difficulty in tracing the firm for whom he worked? Could this be a case of a young man leading a double life?

Simeon P. Fleishman bustled much more vividly from the page. He was a graduate of the Bob Jones University, and, according to the report, 'a highly respected man of God' in the city of Omaha. He had fired the hearts of congregations at the Church of the Risen Jesus by some 'truly inspirational' teaching, and had given some stirring radio addresses which had swelled church funds very satisfyingly. He had invited to the Church 'many of the truly great evangelical preachers of the day, including your own Doctor Paisley', and had served for a spell on the National Council of Non-Denominational Churches. He had also been active

in politics: he had been a leading member of the 'Draft
Reagan' and 'Reagan for President' Committees, and had
chaired a rally which the great man had addressed from
horse-back. He had a fine wife, daughter of a mid-West
preacher, and two fine boys. They had all appeared together
on television, with their dog. Lavish additions were planned
to the church of which Simeon Fleishman was minister,
and also to the extensive dwelling the congregation provided for him. The report concluded: 'The Reverend
Fleishman is a great and active force for good in the
Christian communities of Omaha.'

Oh, God, thought Croft, another committed Christian.
Still, it was easy enough to read between the lines. He had
already marked Fleishman down as a fat cat on the make,
and nothing in the report had led him to alter that opinion.
Not a crook, perhaps, in American terms, for there religion
was business, as business was religion. But still, one used
to sailing on the windy side of the law. Slow but acquisitive,
stupid but cunning. An eye to the main chance – but had
he the ruthless will to seize it by murder? You wouldn't
think it to look at him, but the cliché that almost always re-
validated itself in murder cases was that appearances were
deceptive.

The report on Bente Frøystad was much more dubious
than the first report on Randi Paulsen. It seemed to have
been gleaned mainly from the principal of the theological
college which she had attended for the past few years, and
from which she was shortly to emerge an ordained minister.
There arose from the page a lukewarmness that always
seemed about to change into positive disapproval. The principal had spoken of her intelligence, but this did not seem
to be a quality he prized too highly; he had spoken of her
liveliness, but there seemed to be an implied pursing of the
lips; he had spoken of her modern outlook on her faith,
and here there seemed to be downright disapprobation. He
emphasized that, though free and easy in her attitudes,
there was nothing specific in her behaviour *that he knew of*

that could be objected to, or would suggest her unfitted for her vocation. He thought it very probable (not beyond the bounds of God's infinite grace, translated Croft) that when she had matured a little, and when she had the responsibilities of a parish on her shoulders, her personality would gain in seriousness and moderation. He added that she was an excellent all-round sportswoman, excelling in track-sports and basketball, and a keen fisherwoman.

The second report on Randi Paulsen was very different from the first. A policeman from the nearest largish town described how during her brief incumbency the relations between the practising Christians and the non-practising ones (almost always difficult in small Norwegian communities, and resembling those in the sort of American town where the whites are a smug and confident majority and the blacks a smouldering and resentful minority) had worsened disastrously. Randi had campaigned against the cinema (twice weekly in the local youth club hall, with intervals when the reels were changed) and the dance (on Saturdays, and mentioned only with bated breath by the faithful). On both counts she had won famous victories. Her name stank in the noses of the young people of the area, who meditated various fantastic but vicious plans of revenge. The local weekend drunks similarly bore her no goodwill, and there were one or two teachers in the area (no more than that, for all the schools were overwhelmingly church-dominated, and the non-Christian teachers were almost all those who had lost their faith since their appointment) who resented or ridiculed her activities, and in their feeble way worked against her influence. Her views on sex were puritanical, bordering on the hysterical, but she had found no way to reduce the number of pregnant brides she was forced to marry. She was expected to find some solution to that problem before very long, and it wasn't thought she'd be handing out transistor radios as an inducement.

The policeman was afflicted by the national itch for fairness and middle-of-the-roadery, and in an attempt to redress the balance, if only by a scintilla of favourable comment, he had added that 'local people speak of her as a very clever fisher.' For whatever their religion, Norwegians always have a second God they adore, and that God's name is fresh fish.

The Bishop of Peckham was not pleased. As he walked along the corridor from his bedroom and down the murky steps he cleared his throat in little irritable coughs and rubbed his finger along under his nose. This was always a sign to his servants and subordinate clergymen to stop irritating him and let him have a bit of rest.

He had certainly hoped that this whole business of Ernest Clayton's suspicions had finally been laid to rest, and he had hardly been able to forbear groaning when he found this was not so. On the other hand, he had been lied to, or as good as. The little Ernest Clayton had told him had at least made that much clear. Though he sometimes indulged in the odd innocent sophistication himself, he did not like other people to use them on him. He was a bishop. Like most people who are not too sure of themselves he was very sure of his position, and inclined to wave it at the enemy in moments of stress.

So he was in a far from good mood when he came in to Clayton and Father Anselm in the conference room, and he showed it. They were standing silent and apart, and he looked at them almost balefully.

'This is a sorry state of affairs,' he said tetchily. 'I feel I have been deceived most inexcusably. Of course that is of no great moment as far as I myself am concerned. The point is: the Church itself has been deceived.'

'Perhaps you will sit down?' said Father Anselm, his new urbane tone now become almost silky, his gesture towards the chair ceremonious. As the Bishop eased himself unpropitiated into the chair he added: 'Anger is perhaps not the most profitable emotion at this moment.'

'But perhaps it is the most natural,' said the Bishop

forcefully, almost popping out of his chair again. He gazed at the other two as they sat down like a prime minister about to deliver a rocket to two junior ministers who had expressed doubts as to whether every detail of government policy was divinely inspired. 'Now,' he said commandingly when they had settled, 'let us have your explanation.'

'And pray make it improbable,' echoed Ernest Clayton, but silently. He was still not quite sure that what they were about to get was in fact to be the truth.

Father Anselm, apparently perfectly relaxed in his chair, intertwined his fingers thoughtfully, and gazed at his two inquisitors with his mariner's eyes.

'I think I shall go back, for my beginning, to the circumstances of my coming here,' he said. 'That was very nearly twenty years ago. No doubt you both remember that time very well. The climate of opinion was very different then to what it is today. I mean, of course, the climate of moral opinion.'

All at once Ernest Clayton thought: he's going to tell the truth. And at the very same moment the Bishop's heart sank in apprehension.

'There were, you remember, some notable show trials— I refer of course to trials of homosexuals. And the police were spurred on by the popular press in one of its ugly, self-righteous moods. I'm sure I need not go into detail. The Church, I fear, did not play a very enlightened role in the business. You, My Lord, have made a notable speech on the subject, if I remember rightly, but that was later, much later.'

The Bishop looked as if he regretted that speech now as much as any Festival of Light stalwart could wish him to, but he merely said, rather crossly: 'At the time of which you are speaking I was a simple parish priest. No speech of mine could have had any effect whatsoever on public opinion.'

'Quite,' said Father Anselm smoothly. 'I was not accusing you of moral cowardice. Well, not to go into too many details, it was at this time that I had an urgent need to retire from the world as speedily as possible. To put the matter bluntly, I was told that the police were investigating certain activities of mine.'

'You were tipped off?' asked Ernest Clayton.

'Precisely,' said Father Anselm coolly. 'By a friendly policeman. At that time I certainly didn't anticipate any permanent retirement from the world, but none the less I thought I should make it as apparently permanent as possible. I had always been a devout church-goer, and I had many ecclesiastical contacts. One of them put me in touch with Father Jerome, who was then the head of St Botolph's. In a matter of days I had been interviewed by him and accepted as a novitiate in the order.'

'Wasn't that rather sudden and irregular?' asked the Bishop.

'Not particularly. All the necessary formalities were gone through in the course of time. St Botolph's has always rather prided itself on not being unduly punctilious about such things. Well, as I suppose you will have guessed, I took to the life immediately, as Father Jerome and I had taken immediately to each other. He too was homosexual, of course, though quite unaware of it, and completely lacking in experience. He was a very good man, though terribly incompetent as an administrator. In this respect I could supply what was needed, and he came to rely heavily on me. The other brothers too – if I may be immodest – came to recognize my qualities, and to respect my judgement. That is no doubt why the older of them have accepted so easily the few changes I have made since I took over. In short, Father Jerome recommended me as his successor, spoke of me warmly to the Bishop of Leeds, and when he died about twelve years ago, I was the natural choice to lead the Community.'

Father Anselm's face was angelically clear and untroubled by doubt or guilt. The Bishop's, on the other hand, was furrowed and despondent: his worst apprehensions were being realized; he saw the repercussions of this case spreading further and further outwards, ripples from a dirty pebble, disturbing the whole surface. This could very well become the Church scandal of the century, something that made the Stiffkey affair look like minor comic relief.

'I have always been profoundly grateful for the way in which I entered my vocation,' continued Father Anselm calmly, not apparently noting the Bishop's distress, but noting it. 'In fact, I would go further : Father Jerome was not completely informed of my reasons for wishing to join the order, but he was not completely ignorant of them either, and his action seems to me a model of heroic charity, such as one sees all too rarely in the day-to-day conduct of the Church today.' He paused. 'After I took over as head of the order,' he went on, his voice quite level and his gaze direct, 'I was determined that the Community should follow his example in this respect.'

'You mean you determined to turn the place into a homosexual brothel,' said Ernest Clayton.

'I knew you would assume that,' said Father Anselm calmly. Then he leaned forward, his brown-robed body seeming to regain the old back-bone of steel, and the hard, determined tone entering his voice for the first time during the interview. 'Permit me to say you have a Sunday newspaper mind. You think in terms of wild orgies, "gay" parties, outrageous fun in falsetto voices.' He leant back in his chair again. 'Nothing could be farther from the truth. During my period as head of the order, the Community has been a model of order and discipline. Nothing essential has changed, and the day-to-day life has gone on entirely as before. The spiritual life has flourished, peace and decency have reigned.'

'But the place has become a haven for homosexuals on the run,' said the Bishop, his mouth pursed in prim disapproval. Father Anselm made a pyramid of his fingers and looked at him quizzically.

'You are out of date, my dear Bishop,' he said. 'Homosexuals are hardly on the run these days. Quite the reverse.
It sometimes seems as if it is the heterosexuals who are the
persecuted minority now. But of course it is true that over
the years before I came here I did build up a certain net-
work of friends and acquaintances, and among those are
some – I am very sorry for them – whose tastes run to boys
below the "age of consent", as it's called. Twenty-one!
What an odd age to choose! And sometimes in such cases
we have been able to help – usually temporarily, because
the life here does not suit such, we find.'

Father Anselm's bland irony, coming so soon after his
rebuke of him, irritated Ernest Clayton intensely.

'Then you agree the Community has not been a model
of chastity,' he said.

Father Anselm shrugged. 'What monastery has?' he said.

'The monks here take a vow of chastity,' snapped the
Bishop. 'Will you answer the question properly, please.'

'Times change, My Lord, and the Church must change
with them. You have yourself said the same thing many
times in a much more sophisticated way. What creeds of
the Church are believed *to the letter* in this day and age?
The important thing is not the letter of that vow, but the
spirit. What relationships there have been here have been
conducted with great decorousness: there has been no –
what's the word? – *flaunting*. Quite the reverse. Any sign
of that sort of thing I have crushed as soon as it has reared
its head.'

'You have disgraced the order,' said the Bishop despair-
ingly.

'I have not . . . publicly . . . disgraced the order,' said
Anselm fiercely. 'And in my own view there is not one iota
of private disgrace either.' He calmed down suddenly. 'But
you interrupt. The works of charity, and the provision of
refuge, which I have seen as part of our contribution at the
Community of St Botolph's to the work of the Church,

have rather changed in pattern over the years. For example, in the late sixties and early seventies we had a large number of drug cases – addicts and "pushers" I believe the term is. Perhaps I should add, to forestall Mr Clayton's vivid imagination, that the Community did not become a centre of psychedelic freak-outs, or anything of that kind. We merely provided a refuge for short periods of time, after which, when they considered it safe, the men would emerge into the outside world. Though one or two in fact opted to become full members of the Community. More recently the police, spurred on no doubt by busybodies, well-meaning or otherwise, seem to have turned their attention to sexual matters again. Of course the common-or-garden homosexual like myself is safe enough now, as we have said, but those who put a toe beyond the limits set by the letter of the law have been pursued with extraordinary ferocity. So refugees from this sort of persecution have been on the increase these last few years.'

'No doubt the young man to whom I gave a lift was one such case?' said Ernest Clayton.

'Perhaps we should give him a name. He was called Gareth Clifton-Jones. An old Wykehamist, or so he said. Yes, I believe he was a case in point. I did not ask for details, but while he was closeted with me last night he said something which suggested that he was marginally under the age of consent, and living with a Sunday book-reviewer.'

'You have some sort of secret hiding place, I gather,' said the Bishop sourly.

'Exactly. A kind of priest-hole – a fantasy of our founder, which the original builder very ingeniously complied with. It is a small bedroom, hardly more than a cupboard, leading off from my bedroom through a small opening at the head of my bed, and communicating with the outside through a concealed door in the wall. An extravagant notion for nineteen hundred and eight, I fear : perhaps the good man anticipated an evangelical persecution of Anglo-Catholicism. Even with the present Church hierarchy that seems unlikely. But though there has been no real need for it until now, some of our refugees have lived in mortal terror of the police, and we have put them in there for their own peace of mind.'

'All this is appalling, quite appalling,' murmured the Bishop.

'Not at all,' said Father Anselm forcefully. 'What we have done has been the purest charity.'

'And Brother Dominic?' asked Ernest Clayton, unwilling to be diverted on to questions of ethics before he had heard the complete story.

'Ah, yes, Brother Dominic. Well, as you will have observed, he was still a relatively young man. He came to us first – how long? – five or six years ago. Not a drug case, though. He had had, even by then, a very remarkable career, starting at school. He had been an agent, arranging meetings between clients and attractive boys from the school. Very often I gather the boys were quite unaware they were being used in this way, and quite unaware of the fees Brother Dominic, or Denis Crowther, was collecting. He was an extraordinary young man : quite without emotional involvement; completely efficient; completely ruthless. Though I like to think that the Community managed to soften that last trait a little. After he left school he managed to establish a complete double identity. In his home village he was Denis Crowther, a quiet, unapproachable young man. But throughout the week he was in London, where he managed an extensive service, catering for unusual tastes.'

'Unusual sexual tastes?'

'Precisely. Little boys, unwilling virgins, dwarfs in rubber suits, Australian female swimmers – you know the kind of thing.' The Bishop's eyes nearly popped out of his head at the suggestion. 'Whatever the fancy he prided himself

on being able to provide it, at a price of course. He kept
this going for three or four years, and there must be a lot
of people who regret him today. Many of the tastes he
catered for were quite harmless and legal, but of course
many were not, and in the course of providing for them
he sailed well over the limits of the law's tolerance. That
was the secret of his financial success : he was pricey, but
it was he who took the risks – did the procuring and so on.
Naturally, like all things of that sort the business had a
limited life-span. Somebody peached – for money, perhaps,
or in a spasm of ill-conceived puritanism – and he became
aware that the police were interested in him. If he had been
caught and tried the sentence would have been severe.'

'And so he came here?'

'Exactly. He had, like me, no intention of staying per-
manently. He intended, in fact, to lie low for a spell then
to start the business up again, resume the old contacts, and
so on. But I think the life here suited his temperament : he
was inclined to be rigid and authoritarian, in spite of his
occupation outside the walls. I think basically he despised
his clients and their messy emotional lives. And perhaps the
atmosphere here did some good – it is not for me to say.
Finally he made the decision to make his life within the
walls. He was invaluable as far as I was concerned, both
as friend and assistant. The life here had become a little
wearisome after so many years. He renewed my interest.
He was so good at arranging things too. He managed to
buy a little *pied-à-terre* in London, and we both used it
occasionally, separately. You will have noticed a little car
in the barn. He would take charge while I was away. It
may be the others somewhat resented him : he was not
temperamentally inclined to smooth the edges of authority.
But for me it has been a very happy time. His passing is a
terrible blow.'

'But what attitude did the other brothers take to all this?'
asked Ernest Clayton curiously.

'The first question is how much they knew. They were

tolerant in so far as they had knowledge, which was not very far. Some of the older ones such as Brother Jonathan knew nothing, or so we thought. Perhaps we were wrong : his behaviour when the – women' (sharp intake of breath) 'arrived suggests that this was a culmination of small discontents. Perhaps he'd been wanting to protest at one or two other things for some time but had never been able to collect his wits sufficiently.'

'But the majority of brothers must have known a lot more than that poor old man.'

'They knew more, certainly. You must remember that several of them have arrived here themselves as fugitives from the law. As to the rest, I had made clear to them from the time I took over that, if necessary, the Community should function as some sort of refuge. I persuaded them to take the same view over this as I took myself. They agreed, they even agreed enthusiastically, provided daily life proceeded peacefully and decorously, as it has done. The spiritual life of the Community, as I say, has been in no way impaired. Perhaps there have been what you would call "affairs" between the brothers, but I've no doubt that has always been the case in monasteries everywhere. They have been discreetly conducted here, I assure you of that. As to my excursions beyond the walls, these have always been an occasional necessity, and if they seem to have increased in frequency of late, it has no doubt been put down to the increasing complexity involved in running a community of this kind. You will have noticed that we have fewer brothers than we have room for.'

'Hardly remarkable, in the state of the Church today,' said Clayton.

'No. Nevertheless the fact is I have been very strict in my selection. Any types that seemed likely to cause friction have never been able to get their nose in here. I can truthfully claim there has never been any trouble to speak of in the Community.'

'Hitherto,' said Clayton.

'Quite,' said Father Anselm. 'And I must say I have always regretted the symposia, though it did not seem wise to try to put an end to them. But how right I was. They brought murder here.'

'If, to labour the point again, the murderer was not one of the inmates,' said Ernest Clayton. 'Or, for example, my friend in the priest-hole.'

'But how unlikely that is,' said Father Anselm. 'As far as young Gareth was concerned, I personally ensured that he was locked in with the brothers that night. I was thinking of the women, of course – the young man seemed catholic (if I may so express it) in his tastes, to judge by his experiences. If I had known then what I know now, that the young man was acquainted with one of the delegates, I would have gone further and kept him in the priest-hole. As to the other brothers : this was the one time of the year when concealment was next to impossible. I considered the idea, I confess, but rejected it as far, far too risky. If it had been any of our brothers with a criminal past, he would have chosen any other time of the year. No, the obvious murderer is one of the visitors.'

'But what could be the motive?' asked the Bishop with a pleading undertone to his voice.

'Denis Crowther had several clergymen among his regular clients,' said Father Anselm. 'Needing little boys, mostly, I imagine. One of them, in fact, introduced him here. I have no doubt that it is *there* that the truth lies.'

'You mean they were afraid of exposure?'

'Not altogether a happy way of putting it, but yes : that surely is the obvious motive.'

The Bishop contemplated for some time vagaries of the flesh he had never been greatly troubled by : 'I wonder which of them it could be,' he said at last.

'Any one of them, I've no doubt,' said Father Anselm. 'Including the foreigners if they were sufficiently afraid of their pasts being revealed.'

'You mean you think he tried to blackmail them?' asked Ernest Clayton.

Father Anselm considered. 'That seems unlikely,' he said. 'Possible, of course : our little excursions to the outside world became expensive, inflation being what it is. This had already caused problems. The Community's silver has, I fear, mostly gone to pay for these little luxuries. But he said nothing to me (or I would most certainly have forbidden it) and he was averse to taking risks. I think the mere thought that he *might* attempt blackmail, was in a position to do so, must have been enough to spur someone on to murder him.'

There was a long silence. Both the Bishop and Ernest Clayton believed that they were now as close to the truth as made no difference. But another question was now swimming to the forefront of their minds : the question of what was to be done about the Community of St Botolph's. They were both moderately satisfied Father Anselm was not a murderer. On the other hand he was a – well, perhaps better not put a name to it. They sat for some minutes hunched in thought. It was not difficult for Anselm to read their minds.

'The alternatives are these,' he said, breaking in on their thoughts. 'The first possibility is complete exposure : you go either to the police or to the Church authorities, and you tell them everything I have just told you about what has been going on in the Community. No doubt you are weighing up which of the two to go to, but in fact the result would be the same : the Church would be obliged to communicate their knowledge to the police, and the police would be obliged to tell the Church. There would be – not to put too fine a point on it – a most tremendous stink, a scandal to, almost literally, rock the Church.'

'Not,' said the Bishop, with that note of pleading strong in his voice, 'if all the parties concerned were to act with the utmost discretion.'

'Ah,' said Father Anselm, his voice at its silkiest, 'but they won't.'

'You mean – ?'

'Look at it from my point of view. One certain result of any investigation is that I would be robbed of my position here, and excluded from this or any other order. The first is not important, but the second is. I would be thrown on the dung-heap of the outside world. Rather than that, I would leave tomorrow.'

'But if you did . . .' said the Bishop.

'You may not know it, My Lord, but outside the gates there is a gang of panting, ink-soiled reporters, eager for dirt. I have only to pass the word to one of them, or wend my way to Fleet Street and open communications with one or two papers, and offers will come flooding in : offers of at least four figures, I confidently expect. There are publishers too, respectable publishers, not fringe ones, publishers who would pay well, who would jump at the thing in book form. If I am to become a layman again I shall need money to live in a certain modest style, and to indulge my tastes. That is how I shall get it.'

'But your loyalty to the Church,' said the Bishop feebly. As soon as he had said it he had the sensation of having dug a pit for himself.

'My loyalty is to the Community of St Botolph's, and it will not be I who will destroy it. For the Church hierarchy I feel no loyalty whatsoever. In my dealings with them they have proved shabby, timorous, compromising and time-serving. If they attempt to "clean up" St Botolph's they will bring down on their head a result which their own behaviour has richly deserved.'

The Bishop contemplated the future with his heart in the gravel pits. Ernest Clayton, not altogether unsympathetic to Father Anselm's last remarks, was nevertheless almost as depressed as he considered the force of the man's remarks. If the man did what he was threatening to do, the fall-out would be terrible. The Church would be a laughing-stock and a ruin.'

'You mentioned alternatives,' he said. 'We should at any rate hear the others.'

Father Anselm spread out his hands. 'I am a reasonable man,' he said expansively. 'For myself, I believe that what I have been doing is in no way reprehensible. I hope I have made that much clear. Christ went among the tax-collectors and prostitutes and befriended the outcasts. I have done the same with their modern equivalents. But I can see there may be other points of view – yours, for example – and I am willing to meet you half-way. When this affair is over, well over, it would give me no pain to give up my leadership here and become an ordinary brother. To do it precipitately, so soon after the murder, would certainly cause a scandal, or at least cast the shadow of doubt over my period as head of the order. To do it in a year or two's time would seem only natural, I having borne the burden for so long. In the meanwhile I am willing to forgo my excursions to the outside world and to exercise more prudently (I have no doubt you think prudence a virtue) the shelter I have given here to those who as respectable modern followers of the Lord you think I should shun.'

'But the police – the murder investigation –' said the Bishop.

'I don't think that difficulty is insuperable,' said Father Anselm. 'I personally have every confidence in the police solving the case, at least now that the idiot has been removed. Croft seems extremely competent. I am willing to promise that if they have not arrested anybody within let us say a fortnight, I will go to him. I will tell him that information has come to my ears – through another brother, who must be nameless, in whom he confided – about Brother Dominic's former life in the outside world. That way, you would not be involved at all.'

The Bishop sniffed dubiously at the carrot which that last remark represented. It seemed too good to be true. 'But if Croft does solve the case before then, he is pretty sure to find out about the man's activities,' he said.

'Quite. But as far as we are concerned, he was Denis Crowther, of Little Purlock. We had no knowledge of his other existence, and we are profoundly shocked. I've no doubt, whichever way it goes, I could carry it off.'

They neither of them had any doubts about that. Ernest Clayton had come to have, in the course of the interview, a grudging respect for the man. Of course he was sophistical, Jesuitical, outrageous. He was the archetypal devil quoting scriptures, he was what people meant when they said someone was a politician to his fingertips. And yet . . . and yet . . .

He had made some hits. Against him, Ernest Clayton, he had made some hits. If Clayton was dissatisfied with himself after twenty-five years as a parish priest, was it not partly because he (like the Church which he criticized but followed) had become too respectable, too exclusive, one of an in-group of the lukewarm faithful looking out on the great mass of sinners with an expression of well-bred distaste on their faces? In the Middle Ages the Church had been a sanctuary for wrong-doers: Father Anselm had revived that function. Whatever his motives, were the results entirely to be deplored? Many of the fugitives to whom refuge had been given would today be guilty of no crime. Father Anselm himself would be free to follow his own tastes without interference if he went out into the world again. The law changes slowly, creaking after public opinion, leaving in its wake human wrecks who have been broken for doing what the next generation was to do with complete impunity. Had the Church's role in this been so very heroic? At best it offered some such figure as the Bishop of Peckham, masking his flabbiness with paradox; at worst its leaders poured the oil of cliché over socially troubled waters or tamely followed in the wake of vicious popular prejudices, tentatively wagging their tails.

One thing was certain: if the Bishop of Peckham did not give a resolute no to Father Anselm's second alternative, and give it straightaway, then Anselm would have won.

The Bishop stirred in his chair, and shook himself out of his meditation like a wet dog.

'I think, Clayton, we should go away and talk this thing over,' he said.

'Very well,' said Ernest Clayton.

CHAPTER XVI

BREAKING UP

It was Saturday morning, and Inspector Croft sat in Father Anselm's study, away from the sun, and away from the sight of other human beings. It ought to have concentrated the mind wonderfully, no doubt, being thus shut in in the gloom and forced to focus his thoughts on the case and nothing but the case. But he found it difficult. He would have liked, in fact, to have had a window in the room — a high window whence he might look down on the brothers and the delegates on their last day and see how they were behaving themselves, watch their reactions and the interplay of their characters. For in spite of all the reports and the digging into backgrounds, he felt he knew very little about them.

He could have kept them together longer, of course, but on consideration he had felt he had to let them go. There was very little in the way of solid evidence to connect them rather than the resident brothers with the murder. Their jobs made it unlikely they would stage a sudden disappearance, and Father Anselm's anxiety to have the women within his walls not one minute longer than necessary was, though unstated, patently obvious.

Croft, in spite of his determination that no one was to be implicitly trusted, whatever his position, was nevertheless impressed by Father Anselm: a man of strong will, great capacity. He was impressed too by Anselm's conviction that the murderer was one of the outsiders, though intellectually he could find little to back up that belief. He was impressed by his superb belief in himself. Now that the symposium was breaking up the Community could return to normal, and he could continue his investigations in the dingy familiarity of his own office. Meanwhile the delegates had been given the news of their release from Babylonian captivity, and he wondered how they were taking the news.

As he sat there in the dimly-lit room, with only the crucifix for decoration, he mused on the case and tried to find a shape in it. The pieces in the puzzle shifted around in his mind, coalesced, moved apart and began to form new patterns. What were the pieces? A pathetic, mothered clergyman childishly avid for publicity; a black bishop with one foot in Christianity and the other in a tribal world so strange as to be almost beyond the power of a Westerner to penetrate; a fishing knife; a bitter, rabble-rousing vicar with no rabble to rouse; a leaden American with a sharp financial nose; a blood-stained habit; two Norwegians, totally different in character, both of whom had had lengthy stays in Britain in the past; a sacrificial lamb; an intellectually agile bishop who went flabby in moments of crisis, and seemed to depend heavily on an obscure vicar apparently his intellectual inferior; a shifty-looking brother with restless eyes . . .

The body of Brother Dominic, savagely butchered, his bedclothes thick with his own blood . . .

Two of the pieces started dancing together, and making little patterns of their own, patterns which set up in Croft's mind an insistent series of question-marks.

He wished again he could look at the delegates preparing to leave, and at the brothers preparing to see the last of them.

It was half past ten, and all the delegates had eaten a healthy and hearty breakfast and done their packing. Now they were strolling together for the last time in the sun of another brilliant day, watched from a distance by many of the brothers, drab, uniform, inscrutable. The mood of the delegates had changed once again on the news of their release: now they felt like schoolchildren soon to break up after a rather difficult term. Considering the butchery that had taken place within the walls during their stay there, they were all remarkably spry. Even jolly. The press, clustered around the main door like Neapolitan beggars, had been told that the delegates would be leaving at eleven-thirty. Until then the delegates in question talked, joked and swapped addresses for all the world as if they wanted more to do with each other.

One member had already gone, somewhat under a cloud. The Bishop of Mitabezi had been spirited away during the night, while the press were making themselves odious throughout the saloon bars of Hickley. He had gone in a chauffeur-driven Daimler provided by Church House, and he was even now waiting in the lounge at Heathrow to be wafted back to his own diocese. He stood near the exit gate talking genially to the High Commissioner of his country, looking large, impressive and confident. But he was not talked about by those who remained at St Botolph's. All of them (except Simeon Fleishman) were very liberal in their outlook on race, and deplored discrimination in any shape or form, but they all in practice accepted the idea that different standards had to be adopted with darker skins, and that acts of barbarism or tyranny were best passed over in silence if they happened outside Indo-European boundaries. So the Bishop's surreptitious departure passed without comment, and everyone spoke about almost anything else. Except the hacked-up body of Brother Dominic, which they all had dreamed about these last few nights, some in particularly vivid detail.

Randi Paulsen and Simeon Fleishman exchanged addresses under the trees at the edge of the lawn. Both, unusually, intended to make use of them. Randi plotted extracting money from her church for a lecture tour of Norwegian communities in the States, with 'Woman's Role in the Church Today' as her subject. She knew that any project with 'Woman's Role' in the title could be sure of a grant from some worthy organization or other in her own country.

And it will be so nice to stay with a united Christian family, she said to herself, bestowing her smile like maundy money all over Simeon Fleishman. One does admire a man who has kept the *essential* things of religion so completely in perspective!

Simeon Fleishman had heard that Norway was expensive, and intended keeping all his contacts there polished bright as a new pin. I wonder if she could put us all up, he said to himself.

'To think that all the good that could have come out of this symposium,' he was saying, 'should have been marred.' (He buttonholed Philip Lambton.) 'I was just saying to our friend here how truly tragic to think of all the good that could have come out . . .'

He lumbered on, spreading clichés before him like stepping-stones and then shifting his bulk carefully from one to the other. Philip Lambton was almost dancing with impatience to get away. His young middle-aged body had lightened perceptibly as the time of departure approached, and now that Expectation sat in the air his whole being was athrill to return to a world of motor-bikes and big sound and leather-clad chicks, bearing his Experience, a real murder, to lay as an offering beside their gang knifings and roughings-up. It was as much as he could do to give Simeon Fleishman the seven and a half minutes required to drive the heavy vehicle of his thought to its predictable destination.

The Bishop and Ernest Clayton, as so often before, were talking on the moors. The Bishop had taken Clayton up once more, now that their difficulties had all been apparently solved, and it seemed as if he felt the need to justify his conduct in the whole affair, as if he felt he had been weak, yet couldn't leave anyone else with the impression he had been weak. He enlarged with some eloquence on the consequences of the heroic decision they had taken yesterday, to do nothing at all about the state of affairs at the Community of St Botolph's:

'I think we can be confident,' he said, 'that the situation will right itself quite naturally in the course of events, and then I think we will be able to congratulate ourselves on not taking a precipitate step which would have caused unlimited scandal, harmed many, many people quite unnecessarily, and brought on the Church . . .'

He's done the right deed for the wrong reason, thought Ernest Clayton to himself.

Stewart Phipps said few goodbyes, and those reluctantly. He had formed no bonds in his week at St Botolph's. He never did form bonds. He watched the rest say their farewells with an open sneer on his face, skulking round the outskirts of the lawn, spying on his shadow in the sun, and wondering what issues of public importance had accumulated while he had been away, shut up in this ridiculous place, away from the news-mincers of the BBC, away from petitions and protest marches, away from the stirring calls to arms in the letter columns of *Tribune*.

Bente Frøystad said a happy farewell to everyone. What passed for friendliness was happiness at getting away, but it did. She got caught by Simeon Fleishman ('I was just saying to your fellow-countrywoman how truly tragic . . .') and, squirm as she might, she could not get out of giving him her address. However, when she had written it out for him she explained it was the address of a student hostel, and she had the satisfaction of seeing him crumple it discreetly in his heavy fist after he had left her for someone else. Otherwise she smiled around, frank, open and untroubled, and she was one of those whom almost everyone said goodbye to with a degree of regret.

'Well, this was a turn-up for the book, wasn't it?' she said, with a good attempt at cockney, when she got to Ernest Clayton. 'Wasn't quite the time of prayer, meditation and meaningful discussion that we were banking on, was it?'

'I'm not sure the thing was ever destined to be a great success,' said Ernest Clayton. 'Even before the murder we did seem a rather ill-assorted little bunch, I thought.'

'That was my impression,' said Bente. 'But isn't that always the case when clergymen and such like get together?'

'Well, it is very often so, I'm afraid.'

'That's what I thought. You know, I often look around my fellow students, and think: what are you going to be like in a few years' time? Are you going to be like so-and-so, and so-and-so? – our teachers at college, you know, and some of the big noises in the Church. And you know they are! And then I think: and I've got to mingle with you for the rest of my life!'

'And then?'

'And then I think: Have I chosen the right profession?'

She was obviously serious, but Ernest Clayton was saved from having to give advice by Father Anselm, who emerged from the door of the great hall and stood for a moment surveying them all. In his ordinary brown robe he looked gaunt, impressive, and a little forbidding, just as Ernest Clayton remembered him on the day they had arrived. Then, followed by Brother Hamish, he came forward and went around from delegate to delegate, saying his fare-wells. *Exactly* like end of term, thought Ernest Clayton. And Father Anselm, like any good headmaster, was trying to disguise the fact that he hadn't actually liked many of the boys very much. When he had done the rounds, he turned towards the Bishop, who nodded his head with a mischievous little smile.

'Half past eleven. Time to be off,' said Father Anselm. They all turned towards the main gate and began to shuffle in that direction, somewhat apprehensive at the thought of the reporters.

'No, this way,' called Brother Hamish, and he led the way through the kitchen garden and across to the moors, his watery eyes gleaming, and his cunning face twisted into a smile. They all stepped out after him, and as they neared the wall they noticed a step-ladder leaning against it on their side.

The Bishop of Peckham was almost beside himself with boyish pleasure. '*Isn't* it a good idea?' he said to all and sundry. 'I thought of it myself!' He was very good at executing this sort of notion.

On the far side of the wall, on a rough track a couple of hundred yards aways, stood three undistinguished-looking cars. Propped against the wall stood the bicycle of Stewart Phipps. 'Quickly now,' said the Bishop, and one by one they popped over the wall and hurried over to the cars. In a couple of minutes they were all on their various ways, pedalling or being driven to their various destinations, or to railway stations whence they would be further sorted for delivery by rail, sea and air to their various portions of the globe.

Outside the main gate the reporters stood around. They sweated, undid another button on their shirts, and looked at their watches.

The only member of the symposium not to make his exit in this way was Ernest Clayton. His car was outside the main gate, so anything surreptitious in the way of departure was impossible for him. Father Anselm, generous in victory, had tried to spare him the wrath of the reporters, and had invited him to stay to lunch before he drove back to Lincolnshire, and he had gladly accepted. He watched the three cars and the little figure pedalling savagely disappear in different directions over the moors, and then turned to go for the last time into the Community of St Botolph's.

The shabby little suitcase was packed. The dirty underwear was rolled up in a plastic bag, the flannel and toothbrush and shaving gear were in the toilet bag and tucked into the corner. There was nothing to do now but eat lunch, be friendly to Father Anselm, then brave the reporters and drive off, back to Lincolnshire and the humdrum daily round. Meanwhile he could go out into the sun until lunchtime.

But he did not want to go out into the sun. He alone

of the delegates – the suspects – was left, and now the other faces were out of sight he wanted to sit down and think, quite abstractly, about this murder. Without the human element to intrude, he had an odd idea that the outlines might be clearer.

Ernest Clayton sat down on the bed.

The accepted pattern seemed to be this : Brother Dominic had run a service catering for unusual sexual tastes; one of his clients, coming by chance to St Botolph's, had recognized him and been recognized; fearing blackmail, he or she had murdered him.

He sat back against the wall and contemplated this pattern. It was neat. And yet . . . He remembered the Bishop of Peckham on the moors the next day, his face sagging at the memory, describing the body: 'Dreadful,' he kept saying, seeming nearly to retch with renewed horror. 'He must have been quite frenzied, quite crazed!' Why had the murderer not been neater, calmer, cleaner?

Change the pattern a little, and say that the murderer *had* been blackmailed, that Brother Dominic had already begun to put the pressure on. Did that make the pattern more satisfying? Yes, a little. And yet – in a matter of days, how little pressure could have been applied! But the Bishop had said, 'frenzied . . . crazed.' As a result of months or years of screw-turning, this might be possible. But could a blackmailer work his victim up to such homicidal passion in a mere couple of days?

Look at the pattern again. A slaughtered lamb; a slaughtered brother. Various irrelevant matter presented itself to his mind : *Isaiah* – 'like a lamb to the slaughter'. Brother Dominic must have lain there like a sacrificial victim. 'All we like sheep have gone astray.' One of us most horribly astray. He pulled his sermon-making brain back to the present, and to the pattern : the lamb and the brother.

And no connection between them? None whatsoever?

That was what they had been ignoring. That was what,

sitting back in abstract contemplation, it seemed impossible to swallow. On one and the same night the Bishop of Mitabezi goes out and butchers a lamb, and on the same night, quite independently, one of the delegates creeps down and disembowels Brother Dominic. It was incredible. The coincidence was just too great. They had been so staggered by the horror of the Bishop's action, and perhaps also by the desire politely to ignore it as a temporary aberration, that they had numbed their minds to the fact that these two things could not be entirely unrelated.

But what was the consequence of relating the two things? That they had been too hasty in dismissing the Bishop of Mitabezi as a suspect? The Bishop of Peckham had been very sure that the trance was genuine, but could it have been self-induced after the murder of Dominic? Or what if one of the brothers, or Father Anselm, out on the moors illegally at night should have seen poor Mitabezi at work on the lamb, and taken advantage of it? Or what if one of the delegates had?

Ernest Clayton got up and looked out of his window. The ritual slaughter had taken place at the far corner of the barn, round the front – at the point farthest away from Ernest Clayton's window: he had himself inspected the pool of blood seeping into the earth at that point. From his own window the front of the barn could not be seen – the barn was built at a 45° angle to the guest wing, and he could see only the side and the back. That would mean that only the rooms at the other end of the corridor could possibly get a view of the front of the barn – at most the last three rooms. The room at the far end was Randi Paulsen's, but he felt sure she could be ignored: he had heard the sound of her drawing her wardrobe across the door as he went to the lavatory on the night of the murder. She could hardly have risked pulling it back in the middle of the night. The next two along were Stewart Phipps and Bente Frøystad. Further than that he felt sure he need not go: the next rooms would certainly not get a view of the front of the barn.

Was this the answer: that one of these was meditating *something* – what? revenge? 'vigorous counter-measures'? – and that he or she saw the Bishop at work and decided to seize the opportunity? Accepting this as a hypothesis, he tried to follow it through. Donning a monk's habit (Clayton had heard of the discovery – but where on earth had the murderer got it from? There was none in his room) he or she had crept down the stairs and done the deed. Intending further action to incriminate the Bishop of Mitabezi indisputably in the murder, the killer had first gone out to burn the incriminating habit in the incinerator. He or she had then been prevented from further action by the discovery of the body and the presence of Father Anselm and the Bishop of Peckham around the scene of the crime. The murderer had then been forced to wait outside until – when? – probably until the Bishop and Anselm had discovered the lamb by the barn, or until they had gone to the gate to let in the police. Then he or she had scuttled into the building and gone to their room. The intention of incriminating the Bishop of Mitabezi had thus badly misfired, due to the premature finding of the body and the calling of the police.

He considered this new pattern: did it stand up? Yes, as an outline it did. But only so far, no further, for it took no account of motive, or the murderer's state of mind. The latter could be guessed at from the condition of the victim's body: it was a safe conjecture that after the murder he or she was hardly in a psychological state to carry any plan through coolly.

But who? Ernest Clayton got up, and went into the corridor. There could surely be no objection to his going into the rooms of his fellow delegates, now that they had removed themselves and their belongings from St Botolph's. He walked up the dark corridor towards the stairs, and with an odd mixture of resolution and reluctance he pulled open the third door from the end. The sun, flooding through the window, blinded him for a moment, but when he had blinked he saw in a flash that from this room you could not see the front of the barn. Suddenly he felt very happy. He had not wanted to think Bente Frøystad capable of murder.

He went on, less reluctantly, to Stewart Phipps's room. But here again the drenching sunlight instantly told him he was wrong. It was just not quite possible to see round to the front of the barn. Only if the Bishop of Mitabezi had stood some distance away from the building could Stewart Phipps have seen what he was doing, and this the pool of blood by the barn made certain had not been the case. Ernest Clayton felt well through him a great wave of disappointment : for this knocked his theory on the head. For the life of him he couldn't think up any way Randi Paulsen could alone have shifted that wardrobe silently from across her door.

He strolled nevertheless into her room. From here, yes, one could get a perfectly adequate view of the front of the barn, and the blood-stained corner whence the little lamb had been despatched to find out who made him. And yet – it was impossible !

'It's the only one you can see the barn from,' said a voice from the door. Ernest Clayton, hackles rising, spun round from the window. It was Inspector Croft.

'So I see,' said Clayton. Then, with an unmistakable tinge of disappointment in his voice, he said : 'You had the same idea, did you?'

'Yes, but only a few minutes before you,' said Croft kindly.

'There's no reason to feel disappointed on my part,' said Clayton with a wry smile, 'since the idea was such a dud.'

'And why a dud?'

'Oh – perhaps you hadn't heard,' said Ernest Clayton, rather keen to prove his powers of deduction. 'Miss Paulsen was terribly upset at finding there were no locks on the door, and we had to push this wardrobe in so she could be protected from our rapacious intentions. I suppose she *could* have faked things by pulling it in some other direction, rather than across the door, but I must say I was on my way to the bathroom at the time, and I went past the door: I feel pretty sure she wasn't faking it, and I'm quite sure she couldn't have shifted it silently later.'

Croft paused with an actor's sense of effect.

'There was no need for her to fake it, or move it later at night,' he said. 'You are ignoring one thing.' He went to the door and pushed it open. 'The doors open *out*ward here. She had only to leave a small gap, small enough to squeeze herself out of, and then there would be no need to move the wardrobe again.'

He allowed time for Ernest Clayton to swear silently to himself before throwing open the door of the wardrobe. Piled high on two of the shelves Ernest Clayton saw the brown habits of the monks of St Botolph's.

'And that's what she used to keep the blood off her,' said Croft.

CHAPTER XVII

GOING

LUNCH OVER, Ernest Clayton fetched his suitcase, and together he and Father Anselm strolled out of the Great Hall and across the lawns towards the main gate. Just as at table, with others present, they had talked about anything but the murder, so as they continued out in the sunlight neither seemed particularly anxious to approach the subject both had most in mind.

Putting his little suitcase down for a moment, Ernest Clayton looked around for the last time at the rough stone walls, and the sheep grazing out on the moors. 'It's a lovely place,' he said. 'I can understand your wanting to stay here.'

Father Anselm smiled in his remote way. 'Recent events have certainly cured me of any desire to leave,' he said. 'I shall stay here quite happily until I die.'

Ernest Clayton threw a sideways glance in his direction, and then decided to approach a subject that had been troubling him.

'I remember your saying when you spoke of Father Jerome,' he said, 'how you complemented each other – he other-worldly, spiritual; you the organizer. That seems an ideal arrangement. I wonder whether you and Brother Dominic were not, perhaps, too much . . . *alike*. That's a point which might be worth thinking about when you give any recommendations as to your successor.'

There was no freezing-over of Father Anselm's face. 'That's a very good point,' he said. 'It's something I'll bear in mind.'

They had reached the gate. They turned and shook hands silently, expressing no formal regrets at the parting, then

Father Anselm opened the gate, bowed the Reverend Clayton out, and shut the gate, softly but firmly.

There was by now no great crowd of reporters around the outside of the gate. They had been told of the ruse by which the delegates had escaped their gentle attentions, and they had made a great fuss about ethics, but eventually they had gone off, their tempers ranging from the disgruntled to the bloody-minded, to dip their pens in vitriol and write pieces that went as far as they dared in the direction of murky suggestion and unsubstantiated slur. Only one was left – a dogged little man who made it a principle not to believe a hundred per cent of what he was told, and who had noticed that when all the reporters had charged off in the direction of beer and sandwiches there was still one car left by the gate. The emergence of Ernest Clayton seemed like a reward for his perseverance.

'Have you any statement about the murder?' he asked breathlessly. 'Can you tell our readers what's been going on in there? Would you like to deny some of the rumours?'

'I know nothing about rumours, and I don't see how anything at all reliable could have got out of the Community,' said Ernest Clayton, getting into his car. 'It's not been quite the sort of week I anticipated, of course, but in my profession one learns not to be surprised by anything.'

And he drove off, while the reporter began composing a story for the *Sunday Grub* which began ' "Nothing can surprise me now," said a middle-aged vicar as he emerged dazed and shattered from behind the heavily bolted doors of the murder monastery.'

Driving away over the stupendous purple vulgarity of the moors, and driving resolutely past any would-be hitch-hikers, Ernest Clayton felt more at peace than he had done for a long time. It had been a difficult decision to make, to go along with the Bishop, and it could well be that it had not been the *right* decision – but at any rate it was not the safe, predictable decision. They had chanced their arm, and that in itself was exhilarating. Given the chance again, he hoped he would have the courage to accept Father Anselm's second alternative, and be satisfied with his resignation without sticking out for an ostentatious cleansing of the Augean stables.

Ernest Clayton creased his forehead slightly as he tried to remember the exact wording of Father Anselm's promise to resign.

It was some miles farther down the road before Ernest Clayton began seriously to doubt whether Father Anselm had made any such promise at all.

At the door of the little study which had served as a centre of the murder investigation, Inspector Croft, watched in the background by Sergeant Forsyte, took his leave of Father Anselm. It was odd, but he felt almost apologetic.

'I think it's very likely,' he said, 'that we shan't need to bother you again at all. I hope things will be cleared up in a few days, and I don't at the moment foresee the need for any more work actually within St Botolph's. Of course, there will be an inquest, and eventually there may be a trial . . .'

'Naturally, naturally,' murmured Father Anselm.

'Meanwhile I hope that things will be able to get back to normal reasonably quickly.'

'I hope so. The symposia always cause some disruption to routine, and of course much more so this time.'

'Of course. It must have been a shattering thing to happen, as far as all of you were concerned. Do you in fact find that it is a good idea to combine these symposia with the sort of life you lead here for the rest of the year?'

'No – on the whole I don't,' said Father Anselm firmly. 'I have had my doubts for some time, and I feel sure that after this the Church authorities will raise no objection if from now on we quietly let them lapse.'

'I'm sure that's wise,' said Croft. And then, speaking as one who saw too much of 'the world' and its dingiest side, he added : 'Because I'm sure it is the calm of the life you lead here, left to yourselves, that is really valuable. In your way you seem to me to do very remarkable work. I hope you'll keep it up.'

'I intend to,' said Father Anselm, bowing gravely.

'Sly old fox, that,' said Sergeant Forsyte, as they both withdrew from the presence.

'You really are unpleasantly cynical sometimes, Forsyte,' said Inspector Croft, irritated.

In 'White Gables', Chislehurst, at half past six in the evening, the telephone rang. James Grimwade, just back from the City, in which he was Something, went on calmly chewing his evening meal, but his wife got up to answer it, rather reluctantly : James didn't indulge much in conversation when he got back from the office, but she did like to sit there and see that he got a good meal into him.

She was gone a long while, but James Grimwade, chomping his way through a mixed grill and the *Evening News*, did not notice, or make any attempt to catch what she was saying when her voice floated back from the hall. Eventually she came back into the dining-room, with a very puzzled expression on her face.

'That was funny,' she said.

'What was?' grunted James.

'That. It was the police. They're coming here.'

'Eh?' said James, starting forward out of his lethargy.

'Nothing to do with us,' said his wife soothingly. 'It was about that au pair girl we had – I'd almost forgotten her. You remember, the Norwegian.'

'The lovely Randi?' said James, licking his tongue around his greasy mouth. 'How could I ever forget? The anticipation aroused by the name! The disappointment of the sight of her at the front door! Is she back putting the damper on some other household?'

'No. You remember that time when she went missing for the night, and came back home the next day all hysterical, and swearing she'd been raped?'

'Oh, I remember. Swore she'd been raped but wouldn't go to the police. Don't tell me she's gone along and told them now! She's been a while about it!'

'Don't be silly, Jim. It wasn't like that at all. They were asking me whether anything odd or out of the ordinary happened while she was with us, and I racked my brains and couldn't think of anything. Then suddenly I remembered this, and told them.'

'I don't know that you should have done that,' said James Grimwade. 'After all, it was only her imagination.'

'Well, we don't *know* that, do we?'

'Oh, come on! Wouldn't go to the police – what does it look like, eh?'

'Well, of course that's what we thought at the time. But often they *won't* go to the police. There've been lots of articles about rape recently on the women's pages – it's the in subject – and they all say that.'

'I don't believe a word of it. She just wanted attention, but wasn't willing to make it official. She'd been seeing too many X films – all the films about that time had subjects like that, and her story sounded just as if she'd lifted it from one of them.'

'Randi didn't go to the cinema. She wouldn't even take the children to the revival of *The Sound of Music*. Anyway, what *was* the story? I forget the details. Wasn't it some young man she said she'd met at the SPCK Bookshop, or something?'

'That's it. They'd met there the week before and arranged to meet for coffee. And the story was that he drugged her and took her off somewhere and – wait a bit : didn't she say that it wasn't him that raped her but someone else?'

'That's right – I remember now. It did sound a bit fantastic, I must admit. On the other hand, Jim, you've got to admit that she did *seem* in a terrible state. It took us ages to piece the story together, I remember.'

'But why on earth should it come up again now, for heaven's sake?'

'Goodness knows. But there's a police inspector coming here to ask questions about it. Flying down from the North of England.'

'Good God,' said James Grimwade. 'We'd better sit down over coffee and remember some of the details.'

For some the journey home was almost over. Philip Lambton was in a train nearing Liverpool, where he would find his rectory taken over by a gang of his young friends, complete with their pot, their bikes and their amplifying equipment. Rapture! Stewart Phipps was drawing up outside his front gate, sweaty and nasty after the ride, and within minutes he would find the note on the kitchen table – for the week's rest and spiritual relaxation in congenial surroundings which his bishop had charitably recommended Stewart Phipps to take had served to show his wife just how blissful life could be without him. Simeon Fleishman sat in his hotel in the Arab quarter of London and wondered whether to take advantage of a temporary improvement in the position of sterling against the dollar and cash in all his remaining travellers' cheques.

The Bishop of Peckham, tucked into his taxi and enjoying his first trouble-free sleep for nearly a week, was in a confused dream of enthronement on the highest spire of Canterbury Cathedral, of addresses to the nation which *The Times* would say brought wit and learning back into the Established Church after an absence of three hundred years, and of avuncular bonhomie at Anglican garden-parties with overseas bishops. With a start he jerked himself awake. No. Not overseas bishops.

And on a crowded train to Newcastle, with the glories of Durham Cathedral shrouded in the mist of a hot day glowing in the distance, the two delegates from Norway were nearing the end of the first stage of their journey home. Randi Paulsen had spent most of the trip working out what she would say to her parishioners when she reached Svartøy: 'A *most* unpleasant experience in every

way,' she would say. 'I wouldn't have dreamed it possible.
I think it better *not* to talk about it all.'

Now she was wondering whether she dared sink off into
a little sleep. Sleep had been very difficult recently. When
it had come – and how she had *prayed* for it to come! –
it had been hag-ridden sleep, and always before dawn there
had crept upon her this new nightmare of the man
struggling on the bed as the knife –

She put the thought from her energetically, looked with
polite interest at the landscape, and then, overcome with
tiredness, let her head drop back against the seat.

But when sleep had possessed her for no more than a
few minutes there came upon her not that new nightmare,
but the old one, where she was half awake and half asleep,
and trying desperately to wake, to do something, to resist,
but feeling a great weight of numbness pulling her down,
and knowing that people were around her, near her, touching her, and struggling to open her eyes, to scream, and
feeling a shape, a person, a man, with his face close to hers,
on her, seeing beyond him – the *other* face, that fair-haired
young face, and knowing he was holding her down, and
then trying to scream, trying so hard to scream, and
nothing coming, and feeling –

In her sleep she let out a scream of fear and nausea, and
jerked herself awake. She felt instinctively for the knife she
had kept with her since – and then remembered. Had she
really screamed? Out loud? She looked around the carriage, at Bente Frøystad and the solid Northern families
beginning their holidays; she looked into their eyes and
scanned them for signs that she had given herself away.
Then, seeing nothing, she relaxed the iron rigidity of her
shoulders one iota, and smiled around the compartment
her terrible forgiving smile.

6